This book is due for return o

James Lovegrove lives in Sussex. His first book, THE HOPE, was published in 1990 when he was 23. His adult SF novel DAYS was shortlisted for the Arthur C. Clarke Award for best novel.

Other titles in
THE WEB series

GULLIVERZONE

DREAMCASTLE

UNTOUCHABLE

SPIDERBITE

LIGHTSTORM

SORCERESS

WEBCRASH

CYDONIA

SPINDRIFT

SERIES EDITOR
Simon Spanton

For more information about the books,
competitions and activities, check out our website:
http://www.orionbooks.co.uk/web

THE WEB
COMPUTOPIA

◆

JAMES LOVEGROVE

A Dolphin
Paperback

First published in Great Britain in 1998
as a Dolphin paperback
by Orion Children's Books
a division of the Orion Publishing Group Ltd
Orion House
5 Upper St Martin's Lane
London WC2H 9EA

A catalogue record for this book is available
from the British Library

Typeset at The Spartan Press Ltd,
Lymington, Hants
Printed in Great Britain by
Clays Ltd, St Ives plc

ISBN 1 85881 642 4

CONTENTS

CHAPTER ONE

LORELAND

Jax wasn't all that fond of Loreland.

When it came to entertainment, he preferred Web gamezones that were action-packed – Dreamcastle, for instance, or Draculand.

On schooldays, and particularly on those two days a week when he attended Realworld school, Jax liked nothing better than to suit up afterwards and bat into a gamezone where you didn't have to think or, at any rate, didn't have to think very hard. You had to have quick reflexes to battle dragons or vanquish vampires, but that was all, whereas in Loreland you were required to concentrate all the time, and Jax's brain, weary after a day's learning, often found that a strain.

However, Loreland was Flygirl's favourite gamezone and Jax liked hanging out with Flygirl in the Web. That was why, this evening, he found himself once again in the company of his best and perhaps only friend, roaming among Loreland's cloud-capped castles and yellow-brick roads.

Unfortunately, on this occasion Flygirl had brought along Lioness, who lived next door to her. Lioness thought she was something rather special. She brimmed with pride.

Not only that, she was also one of life's great whingers.

'I *hate* this game,' Lioness said.

Lioness, Flygirl and Jax were passing through a dark,

dense forest when she made this announcement. They were following a winding pathway and taking care not to step on the cracks between the flagstones, since there were bears lurking among the trees who took a particular dislike to anyone who stepped on cracks. Flygirl – an ultravet at Loreland – had advised Jax and Lioness not to stray from the pathway either, no matter what might happen to catch their eye. There were gingerbread cottages in the forest that looked alluring (not to mention tasty) but were home to witches who would attempt to make a pie out of you, and there were picturesque little cottages where wolves dressed as grandmothers waited in bed to mesmerize you with their big eyes, and chomp on you with their big teeth if you failed to answer their questions correctly. The knack to Loreland was remembering all of its many rules and pitfalls. By learning from your mistakes and not repeating them, you were able to get further in the game and survive longer.

'Why do you hate it, Talisa?' Jax asked, using Lioness's Realworld first name rather than her alias because he knew it would annoy her.

'It's all European fairy-tale stuff,' Lioness replied, glaring at Jax. She had altered her features (which, like Flygirl's, were African) using top-grade cosmetic software. Her nose was flattened, her eyes were amber with narrow pupil-slits, and white whisker-like lines scored her cheeks. 'African folklore is much more dangerous and exciting. *This*,' she said, dismissing the forest with an all-encompassing sweep of her hand, 'is for eggs.'

'Is that the real reason?' said Jax. 'Or is it because you're completely six at playing Loreland and you're down to your last life?'

He gestured at the amulet that hung on a chain around Lioness's neck. At the start of a Loreland session, each player was given one of these amulets on which there was a trio of green gemstones representing the player's three lives. Every time you lost a life, a gemstone was removed. Lioness had one left.

'How was I to know that little man in the green jacket was lying about the pot of gold worth 100 points?' Lioness retorted.

'All the phaces in this game are out to trick you, leprechauns included. That's the point. Anyway, you should have held on to his finger and not let go, like Flygirl told you to. Then you would have got the 100 points. And as for stepping on a crack . . .'

Lioness had accidentally done that moments after they had entered the forest. A vast, snarling grizzly bear had lunged out onto the pathway and removed the second gemstone from her amulet with one swipe of its sharp-clawed paw.

'Keep your mind on the game, Jax, or you'll be next,' Flygirl warned. 'You almost stepped on a crack yourself just then.'

Jax, with a surly grimace, returned his attention to where he placed his feet.

A moment later, Flygirl pointed ahead. There were hazy beams of sunlight slanting through the trees, brightening the pathway. 'Nearly there,' she said.

'We ain't outta the woods yet,' Jax said.

Behind the bulbous round lenses of the dark glasses she always wore in the Web, Flygirl rolled her eyes. 'We ain't outta the woods yet,' was the sort of clichéd line you might expect to hear spoken by a tough-guy character in an interactive movie in Hollywoodland. Coming from the lips of a thirteen-year-old boy, even one who hailed from California, it sounded totally gag.

The three of them emerged from the forest into the sunshine. The sun felt warm on their faces after the chilly darkness of the forest.

They found themselves at one end of a green valley. Sheer, craggy mountains rose on both sides. At the far end of the valley, about half a kilometre away, ran a river, spanned by a rickety wooden bridge. There appeared to be no other way out of the valley except by the bridge, so they set off towards it, their feet whisking through daisy-spangled grass.

They hadn't gone more than a hundred metres when Lioness piped up again. 'This is cog. I've a good mind to go bat.'

'Why don't you then?' said Jax irritably. He had had about as much of Lioness's moaning as he could stomach. 'I'm fed up with you egging along with us.'

'I asked Lioness to come with us,' Flygirl reminded him. Her expression, however, suggested that she wished she hadn't.

Flygirl's mother and father couldn't seem to get it into their heads that she didn't like Lioness. Lioness's parents, Mr and Mrs Makeba, and Flygirl's parents got along famously so they naturally assumed that their daughters got along famously, too. At her father's insistence, Flygirl had reluctantly agreed to invite Lioness along on one of her spins into the Web.

'It doesn't matter, anyway,' said Lioness with a regal, dismissive wave. 'We've just signed up with the Net at our house, and there are much better gamezones there.'

'Izzit?' said Jax, using a piece of Zimbabwean slang he had picked up from Flygirl.

Flygirl shot an interested glance at Jax – not because of the slang, but for another reason.

'Yes,' said Lioness. 'I don't suppose either of you has visited the Net brochure site yet, but it's absolutely awesome. Our Net junction-box arrived this morning, as a matter of fact. Unfortunately, we're off to Scotland tomorrow, on a two-week safari, so I won't have a chance to use the box until we get back. Everyone who's anyone is going over to the Net, you know.'

Flygirl was still watching Jax closely. It seemed that Jax wasn't going to let on that he had a certain connection with the Net. A family connection.

'In fact,' said Lioness – now that she had started bragging, it was hard for her to stop – 'I overheard the sales realoe at the brochure site saying to my father that there are places in the Net that are real *utopias*.' She had trouble correctly pronouncing that last, unfamiliar word.

'Utopias?' said Flygirl.

'Yes. I'm not sure what it means, but my father seemed pretty intrigued.'

Jax's face and tone of voice turned sly. 'The Net sounds great. I bet you wish you were there right now, huh, Lioness?'

The words were out of Lioness's mouth before she could stop herself. 'Oh, I wish I was, yes, definitely.'

A fairy with gossamer wings and an acorn-cup hat winked into existence in front of Lioness's nose. Hovering on a blur of gossamer wings, the tiny phace offered Lioness an impish smile and said, in a high-pitched, squeaky voice, 'You have expressed a wish in Loreland. You now have ten seconds to touch wood, or you forfeit a life. Ten. Nine. Eight . . .'

Lioness looked ahead of her, then behind her. They had walked nearly halfway along the valley. The forest was about 250 metres behind them, the wooden bridge a similar distance ahead. There was no other type of wood to be seen, and there was no way, even running, that Lioness would be able to reach either the forest or the bridge in time.

She fixed the fairy with a contemptuous stare and said, 'It's a useless, one-mip game, anyway.'

The fairy counted off the remaining seconds, then

swooped towards Lioness's amulet. It snatched away her third and final gemstone and, with a light tinkling giggle, flew up into the sky.

Lioness dissolved into a spray of millions of fizzing pixels, vanishing.

'That wasn't very nice of you, Jax,' said Flygirl. But she was grinning.

'Serves her right,' Jax replied. 'She shouldn't have started boasting like that.'

'And why didn't you tell her your father owns the Net?'

Jax shrugged. 'Didn't seem important.'

Flygirl eyed Jax carefully. Jax saw his face reflected twice – once in each lens of Flygirl's dark glasses, distorted. The glasses didn't, as dark glasses do in Realworld, shade Flygirl's eyes from bright light. They were a software add-on that enabled her to see visual code in enhanced detail. They were also capable of several other neat tricks.

Finally, Flygirl shook her head, making the beads rattle on her braided hair. 'You're strange, Jerry Hamlyn,' she said.

'You're strange, too, Anita N'Douba. That's why we're friends.'

They laughed.

'Well,' said Flygirl, 'shall we go and see what's waiting for us under that bridge?'

'Betcha it's a troll and it's got a riddle for us,' said Jax.

It *was* a troll and it *did* have a riddle for them. But no sooner had the hairy, malevolent creature crawled out and begun voicing its ritual challenge, than it froze, mid-sentence – and disappeared.

In its place, a d-box shimmered into view.

!!!WARNING!!!
Loreland will shut down in fifteen minutes

for systems analysis.
Please pause your game and exit.

Following the recent worldwide Webcrash, all sites in Webtown were undergoing regular checks to make sure their software was running smoothly and without hitch or glitch. The Webcops had promised that things would be back to normal within a couple of weeks. Until then, Web-users would have to put up with these occasional interruptions.

'Pick up where we left off tomorrow, then?' said Flygirl.

Jax nodded, and they scuttled.

Jax pulled off his gloves, headset and boots, and peeled himself out of his Websuit. The suit was top-of-the-range Gucci-wear, lightweight and comfortable, the best that money could buy.

He hung the suit on its hanger next to his spare Websuit, then exited his padded, windowless Webroom. The door slid shut behind him and the lights turned themselves off automatically. He strode along the corridor, gradually readjusting to the heavy sensation of walking in Real-world. After being in the Web, which gave the illusion of effortless movement, it sometimes took a conscious effort to remind himself how to put one foot in front of the other. Dyson-drones hummed along the floor, veering out of his way as they sucked up dust through their nozzle-snouts.

The corridor linked up with a glassed-in verandah that ran the entire length of one side of the house. Metallic cleaning-slugs clung to the windowpanes, sliding over them in regular patterns, leaving gleaming swathes of polished glass behind. Like the Dyson-drones, the clean-ing-slugs were remote-controlled by the house's central processing unit. The CPU was almost solely responsible for domestic maintenance of the building. It also controlled the climate in each room and monitored security.

Of course, like every other computer in the world, the house's CPU had been affected by the Webcrash. Jax remembered that day clearly. The Dyson-drones had gone haywire, charging around the house trying to vacuum one another. The cleaning-slugs had started climbing the walls. Outside, the solar-powered lawn mower had switched itself on and gone careering around the back lawn, cutting crop-circle patterns in the grass. And all the doors and windows of the house had locked themselves. Jax and his father were trapped inside for several hours, prisoners in their own home, until eventually his father had managed to override the CPU and shut it down.

Looking back, Jax could see the funny side of what had happened. But at the time it had been quite alarming, and for days afterwards he had stepped warily around the domestic appliances, half-fearing that they were suddenly going to go mad again.

The house, a sprawling, one-storey building, stood on the side of a hill overlooking Los Angeles. It was noon, and the sun hung high over the city's grid-pattern layout of palm-fringed streets. It was possible, on this bright April day, to see clear across the city to the Pacific Ocean, which glinted like a huge sapphire on the horizon. A couple of decades ago the sea would have been lost in the pall of pollution that used to hang permanently over LA, but now all that remained of the infamous thick blanket of smog was a faint haze.

Jax glanced out indifferently at the view which he had seen hundreds of times before, then headed along the verandah in the direction of his father's study.

Lioness's remark about *utopias* had got him thinking. He would ask his father what it meant.

But someone else was already in conversation with his

father. As he reached the study door, Jax recognized the voice coming from the other side. The voice was an insinuating nasal drawl that set Jax's teeth on edge. It belonged to J Edgar Glote.

Most people thought Jax's father, multimillionaire Larry Hamlyn, was the man who had created the Net. In fact, Glote was the Net's true inventor. A computer-programming genius, Glote had dreamed up and developed a rival system to the Web that offered improved, more detailed graphics, faster and smoother movement, and a reduction in Websickness which allowed users to stay online up to 15 per cent longer. All Jax's father had done was invest a small fraction of his immense wealth in Glote's fledgling company, Mesh Incorporated.

Hamlyn hadn't been expecting Mesh Inc. to make him very much money. Indeed, quite the reverse. He had bought the company as a tax write-off, thinking it would not survive long. However, since coming onstream three months ago, the Net had surprised everyone – except, perhaps, Glote – by showing nothing but healthy and ever-increasing profits. Although time spent in the Net was more expensive than time spent in the Web, the Net was popular with certain people in the same way that the smarter, flashier makes of car – Ferrari, Rolls Royce, Skoda Excel – were popular with certain people, despite the fact that their batteries ate up electricity and their parts were expensive to replace. The Net cost more to use. It was superior. It had *snob-value*.

Jax halted outside his father's study. He knew it was wrong to eavesdrop but, nonetheless, he put his ear to the door and listened.

' . . . Webcrash was the best damn thing that could have happened to us,' he heard Glote saying to his father. 'A lot of people got a heck of a fright when Webtown went down back in January. They kinda had their confidence shaken, so we couldn't have chosen a better time to launch the Net than the following month. People saw us and thought, "Well, I don't know if I can trust the Web any more. Maybe I should try the Net. It seems safe. It's got a clean track record." And new subscribers have been signing up in their thousands.'

'But surely people realize that if the Net had been online during the Webcrash, it would have been affected, too,' said Hamlyn.

'Maybe so, Larry, but it's all about perception,' replied Glote. 'Doesn't matter what the truth is. The public still *perceives* the Net as being safer than the Web. And that's the angle our marketing people are going to use in our latest advertising campaign. They've come up with a slogan: *The Net – It Won't Let You Down*.'

'Catchy,' said Hamlyn, dryly.

'Isn't it, though?' said Glote. 'Which brings me to my next point. There's been a lot of interest in the Net among the Pacific Rim nations. Taiwan, Japan, Korea – they're all keen to get their hands on our junction-boxes. It's potentially a huge market, and we'd be foolish not to expand into it. It would enlarge our, if you'll excuse the pun, *net profits* considerably.'

'If you think we should, Edgar, then we should.' Hamlyn sounded tired and not at all interested in what his business associate had to say.

Jax became impatient. He couldn't be bothered to wait for Glote to finish. Raising his fist, he knocked on the study door.

'Come in,' said Hamlyn.

Command-recognition software triggered the door's opening mechanism. Jax entered the study.

Hamlyn was sitting in a leather-upholstered chair behind his imposing hardwood desk, on which sat a videophone and a computer terminal. He had his back to the study's windows, through which could be seen a large swimming pool and an expanse of well-tended lawn. Glote was sitting on the other side of the desk, facing Hamlyn. A stainless-steel briefcase rested on the floor at his feet. On the wall behind him hung two original and hugely valuable paintings by Van Gogh.

The bespectacled, ponytailed computer genius greeted Jax as though they were old buddies. 'Jerry! How ya doing, kiddo?'

'Not bad. Mr Glote, could I have a word with my dad, please? In private?'

'Sure, why not? We're about done here anyway. And Jerry, I keep telling you, you must remember to call me Edgar.'

'OK, Mr Glote.'

A hint of a frown flitted across Glote's face. It was like the brief disturbance caused by a breath of wind passing over the surface of an otherwise calm pond. It was short-lived, and Glote's smile quickly returned. But Jax had noticed the frown and was pleased to think that he had managed to annoy Glote, however mildly.

Glote gathered up his briefcase and left the room.

Hamlyn looked across the desk at his son. 'What do you want, Jerry? Is it about that fishing trip again?'

Actually, Jax had not been thinking about the often promised – and just as often postponed – fishing trip, but now that the subject had been raised, it seemed a good idea to try and get his father to fix a date. 'Well, when *are* we going, Dad?'

Hamlyn sighed. 'Soon, son. I've a lot on my plate at the moment.'

'*Dad*. You've been putting it off for months!'

'I know, I know.'

'And my schoolteachers keep going on about the importance of Realworld experiences over Web experiences.'

'Jerry . . .'

'*Your* dad used to take you fishing all the time.'

'He did, but things were different when I was a kid. There wasn't a Web, for one thing.'

'Or a Net,' said Jax, pointedly. 'Maybe I'd be better off going fishing in there.'

Hamlyn leaped to his feet. He strode around the desk until he was standing beside his son. He bent down until their faces were level. His expression, which was usually distracted and preoccupied, had become stern and serious.

'Jerry,' he said, 'listen to me, and listen to me good. Don't go batting into the Net. Don't even joke about it. Got that?'

Jax nodded, perplexed by the sudden change that had come over his father.

'The Net is not the sort of place a boy should visit,' his father continued. 'Do you understand me?' He placed a hand on Jax's shoulder, gripping him tightly enough to hurt. 'Do you understand me?'

Again Jax nodded, just a little scared now.

Hamlyn relaxed his grip. 'Good.'

The v-phone on the desk beeped demandingly. Hamlyn frowned at it. 'I'd better get that,' he said.

Jax nodded, turned, and left the study in a state of some confusion. Just a moment ago he had heard Glote say that the Net was safer than the Web. Yet here was his father suggesting something quite different.

Which of them was right?

CHAPTER TWO

NETSHARKS

Jax headed for the kitchen to fix himself a peanut-butter-and-jam sandwich and to have a good think.

Glote was in the kitchen, sitting on one of the stools at the breakfast bar and taunting Jax's PseudoPup. He had the little animatroid dog's favourite ball in his hand and was pretending to throw it. Each time he swung his arm, the PseudoPup shot off across the floor in the direction it thought the ball would be travelling. When it realized the ball had not been thrown and was still in Glote's hand, it would scrabble to a halt and come scampering back. Frustration was not in the PseudoPup's programming but Jax felt sorry for it all the same. Glote was exploiting its limitless enthusiasm for his own amusement.

Jax summoned the PseudoPup with a whistle. The PseudoPup ran over to him and jumped up against his legs, wagging its tail in demented delight. He stroked its nylon fur and petted it behind its ears.

'A boy and his dog – always a sight that warms my heart,' said Glote. 'Dogs are so adoring, aren't they? Even artificial ones. You can always rely on them for perfect, unconditional affection. Unlike people.'

'Yeah, some people you just can't rely on for anything.'

Jax meant this as a barbed comment on Glote's personality, but Glote chose to interpret it differently.

'Oh now,' he said, 'you and your dad didn't just have a fight, did you?'

'Kinda,' admitted Jax. 'You know that fishing trip he's forever been promising to take me on?'

'He postponed it again.'

Jax nodded.

'I'm sorry to hear it, Jerry. But don't forget, your father's a busy guy, and it's not easy for a man to bring up his son all by himself. And hey!' Glote gestured at the PseudoPup, and then at the kitchen in general, which was large and equipped with all the latest labour-saving gadgets, including a self-stacking dishwasher and an automatic cookie-maker that could produce a dozen different types of cookie at the drop of a hat, turning them out warm and oven-fresh every time. 'This is a heck of a lifestyle you've got going here. You have everything a kid your age could ever want – toys, a fabulous home, even your own Rhodium account at the Days home-shopping site in the Web. You've nothing to complain about. Me, I was brought up in a poor neighbourhood in San Bernardino, one of eight brothers and sisters. My pa was a waste-reclamation engineer, which is a fancy way of saying he worked on a dumpsite. We barely had two cents to rub together. I had to bootstrap myself to where I am today, through sheer hard work. You're a very lucky boy, Jerry.'

'I don't *feel* lucky,' said Jax. He sidled up to the breakfast bar and hoisted himself onto the stool next to Glote's. Much as he disliked Glote, the man was being sympathetic, and just then Jax was in need of a sympathetic ear. 'I mean, Dad has all this money he inherited from my grandparents, and it's a full-time job looking after it. You'd think he could employ someone else to do that for him, so he could spend more time with me, but no-o-o.'

'Your father's wise not to trust anyone else with his money. I think he hopes you'll be just as wise when your turn comes to inherit it.'

'I just wish Mom was still around.'

Jax had been three years old when his mother died, so he had only the vaguest memories of her. He knew what she looked like, because her father kept several framed photographs of her around the house and there was a holo-portrait of her, commissioned from one of America's foremost 3D artists, hanging in the entrance hall. She had been beautiful. What she had been like as a person, however, Jax could not remember.

One thing he did recall about her clearly was the smell of her favourite perfume, rose-water. The smell had lodged in his memory. Whenever he smelled the scent of roses, he immediately felt safe and secure and comforted.

'It'd be nice to have a mom,' he added wistfully.

'Your dad wishes she was still around, too, Jerry. He misses her terribly.'

Glote regarded Jax levelly through the flat lenses of his steel-rimmed spectacles. Nowadays, no one needed spectacles, not when laser surgery could correct any imperfections in vision. Glote, however, chose to wear a pair as a tribute to his personal hero, Bill Gates, the man who, over four decades ago, founded a company called Microsoft that revolutionized computing. By helping to make it easier for different types of computers to talk to one another, Microsoft was instrumental in paving the way for the creation of the Web. Microsoft also made Gates almost unimaginably wealthy.

Gates now lived the life of a recluse in a palatial home which he had built for himself inside a hollowed-out mesa in the Arizona desert. He never went outdoors, and it was rumoured that he had become quite eccentric in his old age. He would, it was said, do anything to avoid spending his fortune unnecessarily, for example walking around with shoeboxes on his feet (packed with tissue-paper for padding) so that he would not wear out the actual shoes that had come in the boxes.

'But you're right,' Glote said. 'Having everything you could want, every *material* thing, means nothing if you don't have a loving parent – someone you can trust, someone you can look up to. Life can seem pretty unfair when you look at it that way.'

'Unfair, yeah,' said Jax, nodding bitterly. Glote was making a lot of sense.

Glote's stainless-steel briefcase was lying flat on the breakfast bar. He reached for it and popped the catches. 'Y'know, there's somewhere you can go where you can even up the unfairness, Jax. Where you can work out all your frustrations.'

'Where?' Jax was so curious to see what was in the briefcase that he did not notice that Glote had addressed him by his nick.

Glote raised the briefcase lid.

Inside, nestling among squiggles of polystyrene-foam packing, was a Net junction-box.

It was a matt-black cube, its edges twenty centimetres long. All of its surfaces were plain and smooth except one, which featured a standard input socket and an output cable. On that same surface the Mesh Inc. corporate logo – the letters *MI* superimposed over a crosshatched square – was stencilled in blue.

'This is the latest version,' said Glote, removing the junction-box from the briefcase. 'The Mark III. The guys in Research and Development are pretty proud of it. It's the smallest model yet, and it's got an awful lot of processing power crammed inside. You can tell just by holding it. Here.' He proffered the box to Jax.

Jax took it from him. 'It's heavy,' he said, cupping the box in both hands.

'It's yours.'

Jax blinked at Glote. 'I'm sorry?'

'I said, it's yours. As in yours to keep. That is, if you want it.'

'You mean, it's mine, and I can use it to access the Net?'

Glote nodded. 'It's initialized for whoever first uses it.'

'But don't I have to subscribe? Sign up? Wait for credit approval?'

'Larry Hamlyn's kid wait for credit approval?' said Glote, chuckling. 'The son of the famous multimillionaire, having to have his finances checked out? I don't think so.'

'I don't know,' said Jax, uncertainly. A thought darted through the back of his mind – a memory of his father's warning: *Don't go batting into the Net.*

'Hey, fine, sure, whatever.' Glote leaned closer to Jax, and lowered his voice. 'But let me just say this. The Net's not policed by Webcops and it doesn't have the usual boring age-restriction protocols. There's some pretty neat stuff in there. *Venomous* stuff, as you kids would say. Games like you wouldn't believe. Zones like you couldn't imagine. Check 'em out for yourself. You'll see. All you have to do is bat in and ask for Davy Jones's Locker.'

Glote closed the briefcase and stood up.

'Anyway,' he said. 'Gotta go. I'm meeting with representatives of a Singapore tech-manufacture conglomerate in an hour. Nice talking with you, Jerry. I feel like you and I have really bonded.'

He tousled Jax's hair. Usually Jax would have hated this, but he was too busy staring at the junction-box to notice, or care.

'I'll see myself out,' said Glote. 'I know the way.' Glote, indeed, was such a frequent visitor to the Hamlyn household that he had his own code-number for the front door and the driveway gates.

Glote strolled out of the kitchen, briefcase under one arm.

Jax sat for several minutes, contemplating the junction-box. The PseudoPup was lying curled up in its basket. It had plugged itself into the mains and was quietly snoozing while its batteries recharged.

At last, Jax got slowly to his feet.

What the heck. It couldn't hurt just to have a peek into the Net.

Could it?

In his Webroom, Jax plugged his Websuit's output cable into the input socket in the junction-box, and plugged the junction-box's cable into his Web-console. Then he suited up as normal. Took a deep breath. Put on his headset.

The world went blue.

Jax was floating. Way above him stretched a glowing field of azure light, patterned with bright ripples like the surface of the ocean viewed from beneath. Way below him lay a ribbed sandy seabed, dotted with wrecked galleons and coral reefs. In front of him, between the surface and the seabed, was a lattice of different-coloured Building Blocks, just like those in the Web, but stacked one on top of another, in tiers, as well as laid out in lines and rows.

The avatars of other Net-users were swimming through the spaces between the Building Blocks, browsing. If the contents of a block took a Net-user's fancy, he or she simply tapped its surface and vanished inside.

Jax was a little disappointed. To judge by first impressions, the only difference between the Net and the Web was the way the Building Blocks were arranged, in three dimensions instead of two, and the fact that you moved around by swimming rather than walking. The clarity of the graphics was perhaps marginally better, but nothing to write home about.

Then he noticed shapes roving around and among the blocks and the swimming avatars. They resembled torpedoes, thick and rounded at one end, tapering to a narrow, crescent-finned tail at the other.

He recognized them from the marine-biology classes he had attended at Webschool.

Sharks.

They moved lazily, propelling themselves with slow, easy lashes of their tails. They turned this way and that, apparently at random, as though casting about for a scent, or a purpose. And, watching them, Jax felt an unpleasant prickling in the pit of his stomach. Something about the shapes of the sharks stirred dread in him. This must have been some ancestral instinct that harked back to the time when mankind first ventured onto the ocean in cockleshell boats; a knowledge – passed down through the generations, imprinted in the genes – that these creatures were to be feared.

Then he recalled hearing somewhere that sharks were the Net's designated phaces. They patrolled the Net, and were on hand at all times to answer queries.

That made him feel a little better. But only a little. In the Web, after all, there were no phaces at the Building Block level. So why were they needed here?

Jax didn't know. But since they *were* here, it seemed like a good idea to take advantage of their presence. He decided to ask one of the NetSharks about Davy Jones's Locker. Spotting a tiger shark nearby, he aimed himself towards it.

He wasn't prepared for what happened next. He hadn't expected motion in the Net to be any different from in the Web, so he was startled by the speed with which he shot forwards. It was as though someone, without his knowledge, had strapped an outboard motor to his back. He found himself accelerating towards the tiger shark at an alarming rate.

He tried braking. Whereas in the Web he would have stopped straightaway, here he only slowed. His momentum

carried him on. He was on a collision course with the
NetShark and could not prevent himself crashing into its
slash-striped flank.

The tiger shark rounded on him, yelling angrily, 'Hey,
buddy!'

Jax's out-of-control progress had been halted by the
impact. Turning himself around, he held up his hands,
palms outwards. 'Sorry. I'm new here. Just getting my
bearings.'

The NetShark scowled at him. Its eyes and mouth were
disturbingly human-like. 'Yeah, well. In future, watch
where you're going, OK?'

'I will. Excuse me, but can I ask you a question?'

The tiger shark grimaced. 'Guess so.'

'I'm looking for Davy Jones's Locker, and I was wonder-
ing—'

Before he could say any more, as if from nowhere another
dozen NetSharks came streaking towards him. Within two
heartbeats, Jax was surrounded by grey, torpedo-shaped
bodies and mirthless, sickle-shaped grins.

The NetSharks circled around him, subjecting him to
intimidating stares and hostile comments.

'Davy Jones's Locker? Ain't no such place.'

'Never heard of it.'

'Dumb kid! He should just curl up.'

'Stupid one-mip smallfry with a big mouth.'

'Get outta here, kid!'

'Yeah, go on. Scram!'

'Go back to the Web where you belong.'

Jax had a good mind to do exactly that. He knew the
NetSharks were only computer constructs, merely software.
He knew that they couldn't actually *harm* him. But, even
knowing this, he was finding their sickle-grins just a little
too sickly, a little too toothsome for comfort. Scuttling
seemed a very appealing prospect. He was just reaching for

the button on his wristpad when yet another NetShark, larger than any of the others, came finning towards him.

The other NetSharks respectfully cleared a path for the new arrival.

Jax identified it as a great white, a species now extinct in Realworld. Its face was oddly familiar, but it took Jax a couple of moments to work out who it looked like.

The great white's features bore a marked resemblance to those of J Edgar Glote.

CHAPTER THREE

UTOPIA

'It's Jax, isn't it?' said the great white. Its voice, too, was similar to Glote's. Jax assumed that Glote himself must have programmed this particular phace, furnishing it with his looks, voice-patterns and even a crude AI replica of his personality. 'Pleased to meetcha. Glad you could make it. Now, what can I do to help?'

'I was told to ask for Davy Jones's Locker,' said Jax, adding quickly, 'but it's not that important. Really. I don't *have* to go there.'

'Sure you do, Jax, sure you do,' said the great white reassuringly. 'That's where all the good stuff is. But you're gonna need the passcode.'

'Which is?'

The great white started to arch and spasm like a cat coughing up a hairball. It retched once, twice, then opened its mouth wide and spat out an octopus.

The octopus floated for a moment, furling and unfurling its tentacles as though to make sure they still worked. Its eyes, on their stubby stalks, looked bemused and bewildered.

Then the great white grabbed one of the octopus's tentacles between its two rows of evilly sharp teeth and bit it off.

The octopus did not seem distressed or alarmed to have been dismembered in this way. In fact, no sooner had the tentacle been bitten off than a new one budded from the stump and began to grow. Within seconds, the octopus had a full set of eight pulpy, sinuous limbs again.

A similar thing happened with the severed tentacle, although in reverse. The octopus had grown a new tentacle, and the tentacle grew a new octopus!

The body appeared first, swelling from the chewed-off end of the tentacle. Eye-stalks popped out on either side of the body, and seven more tentacles sprouted from beneath. In next to no time, there were two identical octopuses floating between Jax and the great white.

'There's your passcode,' said the great white.

The second octopus fondled its way elegantly over to Jax and attached itself to his arm, wrapping its tentacles tight around his wristpad.

'Davy Jones's Locker awaits,' said the great white, with a slow, sly wink.

Jax hesitated. Keen though he was to investigate Davy Jones's Locker, the NetSharks' behaviour had unsettled him. He didn't feel up to exploring the Net further on his own.

'You mind if I take a rain check?' he asked nervously.

'Of all the ungrateful—!' snarled a hammerhead, but it was interrupted by the Glote-like great white, who lashed out with a fin, whacking the hammerhead on its T-shaped nose to silence it.

'Of course we don't mind, Jax,' said the great white, with toothy politeness. 'You visit the Locker when you're good and ready. The octopus will still be on your arm when you next return to the Net.'

Without another word, Jax scuttled, returning himself to the padded confines of his Webroom where he tugged off his headset.

He had to Web round Flygirl.

*

The BiblioTech was vast. No one, not even the librarian-avatars who roamed its aisles, knew precisely how many books it contained. Millions, perhaps billions of them. One copy of every book ever published was filed away here in dusty silence, stacked on shelves that rose more than a hundred metres high, cliffs of words that reached all the way up to the lofty, vaulted ceiling.

The BiblioTech was a shrine to a habit that had nearly died out since the inception of the Web – book reading. Mainly it was visited by old people, who went there out of nostalgia to recapture one of the pleasures of their youth. Some college professors, too, liked to use the BiblioTech for research purposes. Sometimes it was easier to turn up a piece of information there than go trawling through a series of hyperlinked Webtown sites. After all, every scrap of knowledge that had ever been committed to print was available in the BiblioTech, ready to hand.

One of the youngest registered users of the BiblioTech was Anita N'Douba. Flygirl had an enquiring mind, a hunger to seek out facts and answers. If there was something she didn't fully understand, rather than forget about it or pretend it wasn't important, she preferred to go and find out everything she could about it. The BiblioTech was a wonderful place to do that.

She was in the BiblioTech now, looking up the word *utopia*. She had heard the term used before, but since Lioness had mentioned it she had been curious to learn what, precisely, it meant.

A quick check in one of the BiblioTech's dictionaries told her that a utopia was *an imaginary state of ideal perfection*, but Flygirl was not content to leave it at that. The dictionary listed a number of works of literature that dealt with the subject, including the book *Utopia*, written by an Englishman called Sir Thomas More back in 1516, in which the term had been coined. Flygirl made a note of the books' titles and reference numbers in a portable d-pad which she then handed to one of the librarians.

The librarian went away, and returned a few minutes later with an armful of leather-bound volumes.

Flygirl took the books, found herself a lectern and stacked the books on it in a pile. She adjusted a switch on the frame of her dark glasses, setting them to Digest Mode. This meant the glasses would highlight key sentences and passages, so that she could distil the essence of each book in a few minutes. Then she began flicking through the books one by one, rejoicing in the silken ease with which their pages turned.

While she read, every now and then a librarian came by to make sure she wasn't making too much noise and disturbing the other BiblioTech users. The librarians had uniformly stern, pinched faces and wore tweed jackets with leather patches on the elbows. They walked floating a few centimetres off the floor, so that their footsteps did not make a sound. Each kept an index finger permanently extended, ready to raise to his or her lips should a *ssh* be required.

The first book Flygirl went through was the aforementioned *Utopia*. It concerned an island where people lived happy, fulfilled lives, where laws were just, and where everyone behaved fairly towards each other. *Utopia*, in effect, was a blueprint for what the author, Thomas More, considered a perfect society, and it was clear that he had hoped that such a place could exist, and believed that such a place *would* exist if enough people followed the example of the Utopians in the book.

The next book she read was called *Erewhon* by Samuel Butler, and it used the concept of a perfect society to show what its author considered to be wrong with the Victorian society in which he lived. The Erewhonians led apparently idyllic lives, but they were hypocrites. How they acted and what they actually felt inside were two different things. In this way Butler, like More, seemed to be acknowledging that the perfection he was writing about was impossible (*Erewhon*, Flygirl realized, was an anagram of *nowhere*). Nonetheless, he seemed to be hoping to change things just a little with his book.

The third book in the pile was a novel called *Animal Farm* by George Orwell. Its simple story made the point rather well that a utopia was an unrealizable dream.

In the book, a collection of farm animals drove out the cruel, ruthless farmer who had been working them too hard and making their lives a misery. They then set about running the farm themselves, full of high hopes and with every intention of making their working conditions fairer. Eventually, however, the pigs took control of the farm and proved to be just as cruel and ruthless as the farmer had been.

The moral of the story was that the same happens in real life. However hard people try to get along and work together, however hard they try to treat one another as equals, inevitably somebody winds up with more money than the rest, or more power, or both. That was just the way things are – although Orwell evidently wished they weren't.

Flygirl thought *Animal Farm* was a very good novel, and resolved to save up enough pocket-credit to buy a copy from her local branch of Kingston's, the chain of shops in Zimbabwe where these brittle, antique, papery objects were sold, so that she could read the book more thoroughly, at her leisure.

One sentence in *Animal Farm* particularly amused her: "Four legs good, two legs bad." This was a sort of refrain that ran through the book, a chant the animals would repeat to stress how superior they were to humans. It

amused her because a similar convention applied in the
Web, where *eight* legs were good and *six* legs bad.

The next book in the pile was also by Orwell. It was called
Nineteen Eighty-four, and the dictionary had described it as a
*dys*topia, which was the opposite of a utopia, i.e. an
imaginary place where everything was *far from* perfect.
Flygirl didn't, however, get the chance to scan more than
a few pages of it. A discreet cough caught her attention, and
she looked round to find Samuel Jackson standing at her
shoulder.

'Oh,' she said, and looked back down at the book, as if a
visit from the President of the United States of America was
an everyday occurrence.

'Excuse me, ma'am,' said the distinguished-looking
president. In the subdued BiblioTech light, his brown,
bald-shaven scalp gleamed like well-preserved leather.

A couple of nearby librarians turned in his direction and
shushed him.

'Keep the volume down,' Flygirl ordered the president.

'Excuse me, ma'am,' said President Jackson, whispering
this time. 'I've a message for you.'

This was not, of course, the avatar of the real President
Jackson; it was a Web-crawler, sent by Jax to find Flygirl.

One of Jax's more peculiar peccadilloes was his staunch
admiration for the President. Samuel Jackson, in Jax's
opinion, was pretty venomous – for an old guy, that is.
He had brains and attitude, and he didn't take all that
presidential razzmatazz too seriously. Rather than a formal
suit, shirtsleeves, slacks and a beret were his preferred
attire for attending press conferences and White House
briefings, and he had been known to take out foreign
heads of state to fast-food restaurants and get down to
intense political discussions over burgers and fries. But he
could also be impressively statesmanlike when necessary.
At last year's World Peace Day, the twentieth anniversary

of the detonation of the nuclear bomb at Pusan, Jackson had delivered a speech that was a model of controlled, righteous indignation. He had echoed the sentiments of every civilized person on the face of the planet when he had said that if any country ever again deployed a nuclear weapon, the UN would 'strike down upon them with great vengeance and furious anger'. (This was a paraphrase of a line of dialogue famously spoken by the president in an old film he had starred in. It was a reference from the *Book of Ezekiel* in the Bible, slightly amended by the scriptwriter.)

Flygirl knew that Jax's relationship with his father was awkward and strained. She had a theory that Jax looked up to President Jackson as a kind of idealized father-figure, regarding him as the sort of man whose son he would like to be. But whether this was true or not, she had no idea.

Such was Jax's respect for the man, at any rate, that not only did he use his image as a Web-crawler, but he had taken the first syllable of his surname as an alias.

'So what does Jax want?' said Flygirl.

'He'd like you to meet him in Lonelycloud,' said the president. 'Now.'

Flygirl sighed. 'I don't suppose it'll wait.'

'Nuh-uh.' The president shook his head.

Flygirl stuck a *Reserved* tag on her lectern. She would come back and finish the remaining books later. Then she tapped out the code for Lonelycloud on her wristpad.

For the lover of space and solitude, there was only one place in the Web to go – Lonelycloud.

For those who wanted to discuss something in private, without any fear of interruption, there was a zone designed for just that purpose – Lonelycloud.

For anyone who lived in a built-up urban area without

easy access to a park or common, there was a computer-generated land of rolling hills and beautiful vistas that could be visited at any time – Lonelycloud.

In Lonelycloud, you were guaranteed to have the entire zone to yourself, no matter how many other people might also be using it. Parallel-running subroutines meant that, as far as you were concerned, the Lonelycloud you entered was the only Lonelycloud in existence. If you wanted to share it with someone else, all you had to do was log his or her alias in a d-box. When that person arrived, he or she would immediately be transported to your side.

Thus Flygirl, after a split-second of singing blue blankness, found herself standing next to a babbling stream, halfway up a hillside. In front of her lay an expanse of English countryside – rolling fields spread out like a giant picnic-cloth beneath a gorgeous, cloud-puffed sky. The sun was shining, larks were trilling, sheep were grazing in a distant pasture . . . and Jax was sitting on a rock, looking glum and troubled.

'Hi,' he said. 'Thanks for coming.'

'*Ziko ndaba*,' said Flygirl. It meant *no problem*. 'Besides, it was an order from the president. I could hardly say *no*.' She sat down beside Jax. 'Well? What's up?'

Jax took a deep breath and told her everything that had happened since they had parted company in Loreland. He told her about the junction-box that Glote had given him, and about his trip into the Net, and about the NetSharks, and about a place called Davy Jones's Locker, wherever and whatever *that* was. The only thing he omitted to mention was his father's warning not to enter the Net. He didn't mention it because he didn't think it was important. Either his father was mistaken about the Net, or he had simply been trying to stop Jax having any fun. Both explanations seemed equally likely, to Jax.

'Davy Jones's Locker,' said Flygirl. 'In the olden days, sailors used to say that was the place where people who drowned at sea went. It's a sort of graveyard for dead seamen.'

'So who was Davy Jones?' Jax enquired.

'If I remember correctly, that's what sailors used to call the Devil,' said Flygirl. 'Much less of a mouthful than *Beelzebub*,' she added.

Jax laughed, but at the same time he couldn't suppress a small shiver. It seemed a bit creepy, to name a Net zone after a graveyard owned by the Devil.

'Anyway, don't you want to know what I've been up to?' Flygirl asked.

'Sure,' said Jax. 'What have you been up to?'

Flygirl told him what she had learned about utopias. 'Maybe,' she said, 'this Davy Jones's Locker is where we'll find them.'

'Maybe,' said Jax. 'It's worth a look, at any rate. I'd have gone there myself, of course, only I'm—'

'Too much of a coward?' Flygirl suggested, with a teasing smile.

'No,' said Jax emphatically, although there was a lot of truth in what she had said. 'I just thought you'd like to come with me. We do most things together, after all.'

'Well, Jax . . .' Flygirl drummed her fingers against her chin. 'I suppose I could come with you into the Net. Hold your hand so you won't get scared.'

Jax flashed her an annoyed look, which she ignored.

'There's just one small problem.'

'What?'

'I don't have a junction-box, you one-mip!'

Jax grinned. For once in his life, he was a step ahead of Flygirl. 'Aha! You see, I've thought about that. Your friend Lioness—'

Now it was Flygirl's turn to be annoyed. 'She's *not* my friend.'

'OK, OK. But she *is* your next-door neighbour, and she *does* have a junction-box.'

'And you want me to go round to her house and ask to borrow it, is that what you're saying?'

'Yeah.'

Flygirl waved a hand. 'No way. Forget it. Curl up. Never in a million years. I wouldn't ask Talisa Makeba to lend me a *toothpick*.'

'Well, then,' said Jax, 'how about this? She's going away on vacation tomorrow, right? Scotland, with her parents, to see the wolves and the big cats and the genetically-engineered loch monsters. There'll be no one in the house. You could just—' He left the rest unsaid.

Flygirl thought hard. She had to admit she was extremely curious to take a look in the Net. The utopias that Lioness had referred to – what *were* they? What *were* these places of perfection that the Net, allegedly, contained? Flygirl's enquiring mind – that restless hunger of hers for facts, for morsels of information, for *flies* – had not been wholly satisfied by her trip to the BiblioTech. There was more to be learned, and the answers, it seemed, might be found in the Net.

Her parents and the Makebas had key-cards for each other's houses so that while one family was away, the other could check up on their property, make sure everything was all right, turn on lights to deter burglars, and so on. She knew where the key-card was kept. She could nip in and out of the Makebas' house without any difficulty. She could use the junction-box, and no one would be any the wiser. Yes—

'Yes,' she said. 'Let's do it.'

'All right!' exclaimed Jax, and he punched the air.

They made a plan. Tomorrow evening, Flygirl would go

round to the Makebas'. Then she and Jax would meet in the Net to find out what lay in the mysterious Davy Jones's Locker.

CHAPTER FOUR

GUARD HYENA

The following night, shortly after sunset, Flygirl removed the Makebas' key-card from its hiding-place inside the mouth of the Shona tribal mask that hung as decoration in her parents' hallway. She slipped the key-card into the pocket of her jeans and let herself out of the house, quietly easing the front door shut behind her with a soft click.

She stole across the garden to the front gate, avoiding the gravel driveway and keeping to the grass. She had told her parents that she was going to spin into the Web for the next couple of hours, which, while it wasn't exactly the truth, wasn't exactly a lie either. She just hadn't specified whose bedroom she was going to be in and whose Websuit she would be using.

The N'Doubas lived in Belgravia, a well-to-do suburb of Harare, the capital of Zimbabwe. Every home in the suburb was set in its own grounds, with security gates and high walls around the garden. While Harare was by no means as dangerous a place to live in as it had been at the end of the previous century when crime had been rife on its streets, it was still far from being the safest city on earth. The discovery, a decade ago, of several new and extensive gold fields in the country's eastern region had brought about an upturn in Zimbabwe's economic fortunes (gold-plated wiring, disks and circuitry being vital components of Web technology), and with this prosperity had come the peace and political stability which Zimbabweans had long craved. However, the new wealth had yet to filter all the way down to the lowest levels of Zimbabwean society, so there remained – especially in the cities – a restless, unhappy underclass who, lacking money and decent housing, looked with an envious eye on the better-off, on those who had what they did not have. Hence people with respectable incomes, such as Dr and Mrs N'Douba, still had to take care to protect their property and possessions.

Flygirl unlocked the front gate with her own key-card and stepped cautiously out onto the avenue which was lined with jacarandas and acacias. The avenue was deserted, and the blossom-heavy boughs of the trees swayed and sighed in a gentle, cool breeze. The clear night sky scintillated with stars, and crickets sang, their voices competing with the distant whirring hum of the condensation plants which were located over in the Highlands district of the city. From where she was standing, Flygirl could see the tops of the condensation plants' funnel-shaped towers, adorned with flashing red aircraft-warning lights. Like most of southern Africa, Zimbabwe had been suffering a continuous, relentless drought since the end of the previous century. The towers extracted moisture from the air, working through the cool of the night to supply the citizens of Harare with all the fresh water they needed for the following day.

It was just over a hundred metres from the N'Doubas' front gate to the Makebas'. Flygirl made her way along the pavement, keeping close to the wall and casting frequent glances over her shoulder. It was not wise to venture out after dark on foot, even if you had only a short distance to travel.

Reaching the Makebas' gate, she hurriedly inserted the key-card into the slot in the metal plate that was set into the gatepost.

Nothing happened. The lock on the gate did not open.

She muttered a curse under her breath and tried the key-card again.

Still the lock did not open.

She glanced at her wristwatch. Quarter to eight. Over in California Jax would be waiting, suited up, ready to bat in. They had agreed to rendezvous in the Net at eight p.m. her time (ten in the morning, Pacific Coast Time). Jax was counting on her to be there, and she had failed him at the first obstacle. She couldn't even get into the Makebas' house!

Then she realized why the key-card wasn't working. It was her own key-card, which only worked for her parents' house. The two key-cards looked exactly alike – plain grey wafers of plastic with a chip embedded in one side. They had both been in her jeans pocket, and she had got them mixed up.

Tutting at her carelessness, Flygirl swapped cards and inserted the right one.

The gate unlocked itself with a soft clank. She swung the gate open, stepped through, and closed it behind her.

All was shadowy and still in the Makebas' garden. The house loomed ahead, its whitewashed walls glowing palely in the moonlight, its windows empty black rectangles. A huge baobab tree stood in front, partly obscuring the house with its squat, knobbly trunk and thick branches.

The driveway that curved up to the front door was brick-paved, not gravelled. Flygirl began walking along it. She was wearing trainers, so her footsteps were all but silent. It occurred to her that she ought to avoid stepping on the cracks between the bricks, so that a bear would not leap out from one of the thickets of poinsettia or from behind one of the towering, cactus-like euphorbias that grew on either side of the driveway. Then she realized how absurd that was. She wasn't in Loreland now and, anyway, unless she went on tiptoes like a ballerina, there was no way she could avoid stepping on the cracks between the bricks. And – more to the point – there were no bears, or any other kinds of wild beasts, in the Makebas' garden!

A soft, wheezy chuckling from somewhere nearby brought Flygirl to a halt. She peered, big-eyed, in the direction from which the sound had come. All she could see was the leafy black silhouette of a poinsettia bush. She breathed shallowly, waiting for the sound to repeat itself, praying it would not. She hoped her ears had been playing tricks on her and that she had mistaken a perfectly innocent noise for something not so innocent. Perhaps it had just been some small nocturnal mammal snuffling around beneath the poinsettia. Yes. Perhaps.

Several further seconds passed before Flygirl was able to convince herself to start walking again. She told herself she had been fretting over nothing.

Then the noise came again.

There was a boy in Flygirl's class at Realworld school who suffered from asthma. Sometimes when he laughed, it sounded like he had thistles stuck in his throat.

This noise was similar, a whistling, wheezy *heh heh heh*.

Flygirl looked again at the poinsettia bush, and this time saw a pair of eyes staring at her. Glowing, yellowy eyes.

And then the creature that owned the eyes came slouching out from the shadow of the bush into the moonlight.

It looked a little like a dog, but its shoulders were higher and its haunches lower than those of an ordinary canine. It had rounded ears and a spotted pelt, and stood with its tail curled under its belly and its broad flat head hunched down, as though it was cowering. But it was not cowering. It was grinning at Flygirl, its tongue lolling floppily out between its wicked arrays of teeth, and as it regarded her with those large, bright, baleful eyes, it snickered again. Hungrily.

A hyena.

Flygirl didn't need to ask herself what a lone hyena was doing inside the Makebas' compound. All over Africa, hyenas were being bred and trained for use as guard dogs. They were cunning, which made them less predictable – and so more dangerous – than the traditional breeds of guard dog such as the Alsatian or the Doberman. They were also just as ferocious. If you were going to be away from home for a while, it didn't cost much to hire a guard hyena from a professional security firm to patrol your premises. This, evidently, was what the Makebas had done.

No doubt Flygirl's parents had known about the presence of the guard hyena in the Makebas' garden. If only she had told them where she was going.

But it was too late to think about that now.

The hyena took another couple of paces towards Flygirl. A glistening strand of drool leaked down from one corner of its jaws.

Flygirl glanced over to the door of the house. She could run to it, but even if she got there before the hyena did (which was unlikely), the hyena would catch up with her while she was trying to open the door with the key-card. The same thing would happen if she made for the front gate.

There was nowhere she could run to. No safe refuge.

Except . . .

Her legs started moving even before the idea had fully formed in her brain. It was as though her body knew before her mind did that she had only one chance to escape the hyena and if she didn't seize it now, it would be lost for ever.

She sprinted for the baobab tree. Out of the corner of one eye she saw the guard hyena take off after her, pursuing her with the loping, lolloping gait that was characteristic of its species. Flygirl ran faster, her feet thumping on the lawn, her heart thumping in her chest.

As she came closer to the baobab, she scanned its trunk for handholds. Its bark was smooth, but lumps protruded here and there.

She could hear the guard hyena behind – gaining on her rapidly.

A dozen paces to the baobab tree.

Half a dozen.

She thought she could feel the hyena's breath on the backs of her legs.

And then she was leaping.

And climbing, picking her way up the side of the baobab as surefootedly as though she were a real fly, not simply a Flygirl. Panic lent her speed and agility. Within seconds she reached one of the baobab's lower branches, a feat which under any other circumstances would probably have been beyond her.

The guard hyena jumped up after her, snarling and snapping. Its gnashing teeth missed her heels by centimetres. The hyena went skidding back down the trunk and crashed to the ground, rolling onto its back. Immediately getting back on its feet, it launched itself at the tree again, leaving dozens of shallow gouges in the bark as it tried to claw its way up, but again, without success.

It tried once more, and failed, then settled down on its haunches and stared resentfully up at Flygirl, who was by now lying prone along the branch, hugging it tightly with her arms and legs. She could see the hyena thinking hard, trying to figure out how it might get to her. Hyenas, it appeared, could not climb trees, so as long as she remained where she was, she would be all right.

But she couldn't stay up there for ever. Sooner or later, for one reason or another, she would have to come down.

Damn Jax! This was all his fault.

There was nothing else for it, she was going to have to shout for help. Her parents would hear her cries. They would call the police who would come with animal-handlers to catch the hyena.

And then, of course, she would have to explain to her parents – *and* to the police – what she had been doing in the Makebas' garden, trespassing on their private property. The police would most likely let her off with a caution, but her parents . . . Her parents would be furious. She would be grounded for life, probably. Her father would get hold of a W-chip that would prevent her from visiting anything other than educational sites in Webtown. She would never see Jax again!

Actually, given how she was feeling about Jax just then, never seeing him again might not be a bad thing. For *his* sake.

She turned her head in the direction of her parents' house, ready to start shouting. It was then she noticed that one of the baobab's branches, slightly higher up than the one to which she was clinging, extended almost to the wall that divided the Makebas' garden from her own.

Flygirl could hardly believe her luck. The wall wasn't much more than three metres tall. She could reach the top of it from the branch, and then could lower herself over the other side and drop down into her own garden. If her memory served, there was a shrub bed at the foot of the wall on the other side – a nice, soft landing. She could get back home, and no one would ever have to know where she had been.

She got slowly to her feet, holding onto another branch for balance. The guard hyena got to its feet, too, cocking its head in curiosity. What was the human in the tree up to?

The baobab's branches spread out like the spokes of a wheel, at evenly-spaced intervals. Flygirl began climbing cautiously round from one to the next. The hyena followed her on the ground, tracking her progress. Much though she wanted to be out of the Makebas' garden as quickly as possible, Flygirl knew she must not hurry. One mistake – a misplaced foot, an insecure handhold – and she would fall, and that would be that.

At last she reached the branch she wanted to be on. It looked sturdy. She straddled it, legs dangling, and began shunt-shuffling herself along. The hyena prowled below her, slavering and licking its chops. No doubt it was praying to the god of hyenas, begging for some accident to befall the human.

The god of hyenas must have been listening.

Halfway along the branch, Flygirl heard a deep, low creak and felt the branch shudder between her thighs.

It's going to be all right, she told herself. The tree's old, but the branch is thick and strong, and I don't weigh much. Well, not *that* much.

She continued shunt-shuffling along. The branch continued to creak and shudder. Then it began to groan.

The guard hyena cackled eagerly.

Flygirl was within a metre of the wall and getting ready to leap for it when, with a loud, rending *creee-eeack*, the branch broke away from the baobab's trunk.

The next thing Flygirl knew, she and the branch were plummeting to earth.

CHAPTER FIVE

DAVY JONES'S LOCKER

Flygirl lay on her back on the ground, stunned. Now she understood what was meant when people who had received a knock on the head were said to *see stars*. For here, filling her vision, were stars. Hundreds of them.

It took her a few moments to realize that they were real stars, the ones you traditionally see at night.

Then she recalled where she was and what had just happened.

The hyena!

She struggled to sit up, but none of her limbs seemed to work properly. Her arms flailed uselessly around, her feet dug futile grooves in the grass.

At any moment, she expected to hear the hyena's asthmatic snickering right beside her ear, and to feel sharp teeth sinking into her throat, perhaps, or her stomach.

Still, she kept trying to sit up and, eventually, something came of her frantic efforts. She managed to push herself up into a kind of reclining position, then roll herself fully onto her side.

She was lying next to the branch. She looked around for the hyena. It was lying three metres away, sprawled beneath the branch. The branch had crushed it, flattening its torso in the middle. The hyena's forelegs were twitching, but it was quite dead.

Slowly, Flygirl got to her feet. She inspected herself all

over. Apart from a few bruises, she was unhurt. She had had a lucky escape.

She looked up at the baobab. There was a great pale scar on its trunk where the branch had torn away. With any luck the Makebas would think it had broken off of its own accord, and that the guard hyena had simply had the misfortune to be underneath at the time.

She consulted her watch. Ten to eight. Just five minutes had elapsed since she had entered the garden. She felt as if she had lived several lifetimes in those few minutes.

Jax would still be expecting to meet her in the Net. She was tempted not to keep their rendezvous. Jax, after all, was to blame for all of this. But she decided she couldn't let the stupid one-mip bat into the Net without her. Who knew what trouble he might get himself into!

She took one last glance at the hyena, which was now lying completely still. She felt rather sorry for the poor creature, now that it wasn't trying to bite her.

She set off towards the house.

At the front door she let herself in using the key-card. She didn't turn on any lights inside. There was a chance that her parents might see them and alert the police.

She had been in the Makebas' house a number of times before, most recently for Lioness's thirteenth birthday party. Most kids were content to hold their birthday parties in the Web, but not Lioness. Oh no. She had insisted on a full traditional Realworld celebration, complete with cake and games and a juggler and musicians and an inflatable bouncy castle on the lawn. And, Flygirl had to admit, as parties went it had been quite a success. Lioness had lorded it over everyone, of course, organizing the games and generally acting as though she were a queen and all the guests were her subjects. But apart from that the occasion, in its old-fashioned way, had been novel and interesting.

Flygirl groped her way through the darkened house, moonlight her only illumination. She found her way to Lioness's bedroom. Lioness did not have a Webroom – her parents weren't *that* rich – but she did have a top-of-the-line Websuit, a Calvin Klein, tailor-made for her in a spangly, shocking-pink material. Her Net junction-box was plugged in, ready for use.

Flygirl wriggled herself into Lioness's Websuit and zipped it up. It was roomier than her own Websuit, especially around the hips and backside, which pleased her immensely.

'OK, Jax,' she said, lowering the hood over her head. 'Here I come.'

They spun in almost simultaneously at a prearranged entry-point in the Net's Building Block level.

Immediately, Flygirl pointed at Jax's forearm and said, 'What's that?'

Jax glanced down at the octopus that was still attached to his left arm as the great white had said it would be.

'Passcode to Davy Jones's Locker,' he told her.

'You never said anything about needing a passcode.'

'Didn't I? Guess I forgot.'

'I don't believe it!' Flygirl was furious. 'Do you have any idea what I had to go through to get here, Jax? Do you? I was nearly killed. Twice! And now, after all that, you tell me I'm not going to be able to get into Davy Jones's Locker!'

'Killed?'

Flygirl, tight-lipped, explained about her encounter with the guard hyena.

'Well, I'm sorry,' said Jax, 'but I could hardly have known, could I? Anyway, the main thing is that you're OK. And as for getting you a passcode – *ziko ndaba*. Watch.'

He unpicked one of the octopus's tentacles from his

arm. Taking a firm grip on the pulpy limb, he wrenched it off.

'Sus!' said Flygirl, wincing. (*Sus* was Zimbabwean slang for *gag*.)

'Don't worry. It's all right. See?'

As before, the octopus re-grew its missing tentacle, and the tentacle sprouted a brand new octopus.

'Self-replicating software,' said Flygirl, nodding in approval. '*Snice*.' (*Snice* meant the opposite of *sus*.)

Jax held the new octopus out to Flygirl, and she let it wrap its tentacles around her arm.

'So now what do we do?' she said. For the first time since arriving in the Net, she took stock of her surroundings. Turning herself around in the water, she noticed that her movements seemed a little sluggish. She also became aware that she couldn't feel anything around her waist and hips. At first she thought there must be some funnel in Lioness's Net junction-box, but then she realized that in fact the problems were being caused by Lioness's Websuit. Because the Websuit didn't fit *her* perfectly, it wasn't giving her full interface with the Net. Websuits needed to be snug-fitting in order to work properly.

'Is Davy Jones's Locker in one of those, do you think?' she said to Jax, indicating the three-dimensional lattice of Building Blocks.

'Probably. Maybe we should ask one of the NetSharks.' Jax said this reluctantly.

'Maybe,' said Flygirl. 'Or maybe the octopuses know what to do. They look pretty intelligent.'

'That's a good idea,' said Jax, relieved. The prospect of talking to one of the Net's bad-tempered phaces again had not appealed to him. 'I hadn't thought of that.'

'You never do,' said Flygirl. 'That's why I'm the brains of this outfit.'

She brought the octopus up close to her face and looked

it square in the eye. 'Would you show us the way to Davy Jones's Locker, please?'

The octopus flattened itself against her arm, tensed, then thrust away with all its might, but still keeping its grip on Flygirl so that she was yanked along behind it in a swirl of silvery bubbles. For something so small, the octopus was deceptively strong. With a single succulent throb of its body it was able to propel both itself and Flygirl a good ten metres.

Without having to be asked to, Jax's octopus did the same. They both found themselves being tugged along by their left arms in a series of jerky ten-metre lunges.

The octopuses dragged them downwards. The galleons and reefs on the seabed loomed closer. Soon Jax and Flygirl were moving horizontally over the sand, with seaweed fronds slithering against their bodies and startled crabs scuttling out of their way.

They were drawn by the octopuses under the Building Blocks. The water was darker beneath the lattice of huge, coloured cubes, and there were strange sea creatures here that neither of the children recognized. Hideous skeletal things, like X-rays of fish. Blind white worms that writhed along the sand. Transparent jellyfish with arrays of glowing lights all over their bodies.

Then, ahead, Jax and Flygirl spotted a huge outgrowth of pink coral rising from the seabed. The outgrowth was roughly cube-shaped, and the coral's fronds were woven so densely together that they formed an apparently im-penetrable surface.

The octopuses headed for the outgrowth and with one last powerful pulse of their bodies they brought Jax and Flygirl's left hands into contact with the coral's surface.

There was a moment of blue-and-tone, then Jax and Flygirl found themselves in a large undersea cavern the size of a ballroom. Illumination was provided by phosphorescent algae which coated the cavern's walls, floors and roof, giving off a glimmering blue glow. The octopuses remained attached to their arms.

The cavern was empty apart from a pirates' treasure chest which sat at its centre on a raised section of the floor. The wood of the chest was old and rotten, its brass fittings were tarnished, and it was fitted with a large padlock of a type neither Jax nor Flygirl had ever seen before. Rather than a single keyhole, the padlock had eight round openings arranged in a circle. Both Jax and Flygirl wondered what sort of key was required to open it.

The answer was, not a key at all, but an eight-limbed cephalopod.

Flygirl's octopus detached itself from her arm and swam over to the padlock. Inserting the tips of its tentacles into the eight holes, it performed a complicated twisting manoeuvre. The padlock came undone, and the octopus withdrew its tentacles and dextrously removed the padlock from the treasure chest's hasp.

Jax's octopus let go of his arm and joined the other one at the chest. First it lifted the hasp, then together the two octopuses raised the lid.

A bright blue light – far brighter than the glow of the phosphorescent algae – flooded out from the opened chest.

Jax and Flygirl shut their eyes against the light. Both heard the familiar brief tone that always accompanied a bat between sites in the Web.

Then they were somewhere warm and humid.

They opened their eyes.

They were in a tropical jungle. Overhead, palm-tree leaves were laced together tightly, forming a dense green canopy. Thick thickets of bamboo clustered all around them. Warbling birdsong filled the air. Insects chirruped and buzzed.

'Hmph,' said Jax, glancing around, unimpressed. 'I was expecting a bit more.'

'Me, too,' said Flygirl. 'Good sound quality, though.' She bent forward to inspect the bark of one of the palms, setting the mode-switch on her dark glasses to Magnification/ Enhancement. 'And the graphics textures aren't bad, either. But if this is supposed to be a utopia—'

Jax finished the sentence for her. 'It's not very imaginative. Nothing you wouldn't find in a vacation zone in the Web.'

'Perhaps we ought to explore the place a bit before we write it off completely,' Flygirl suggested.

Before Jax could reply, they heard crashing and shouting coming from not far away.

'What on earth is *that*?' said Jax.

'See that kopje over there?' Flygirl pointed to a large outcrop of rock the summit of which rose above the tops of the trees. 'If we climb that, maybe we'll be able to get a better view of what's going on.'

They scrambled up the side of the rock outcrop, Flygirl lagging slightly behind Jax because of the looseness of Lioness's Websuit. Shortly, they both emerged above the trees into clear sunlight. The jungle spread as far as the eye could see in all directions. The sun was an ordinary sun and beat down with a fierce tropical heat, but the sky in which it shone was weird. It was not a smooth, even blue, like the sky in the Web or Realworld. Rather it was the rippled, flexing blue of the sea-surface that stretched over the Net's Building Blocks.

The shouting and crashing got louder. Between breaks in the jungle canopy they caught glimpses of men and women dressed in khaki safari suits and pith helmets. They were running, apparently chasing something, but neither of the children could see what it was.

Jax noticed that the men and women were carrying rifles.

'Hunters,' Flygirl said, her lip curling in sour disapproval. 'We're not supposed to be here, Jax. This is a grown-ups' zone.'

Not far from the rock outcrop there was a large clearing. From their vantage point, crouching on the outcrop's summit, Jax and Flygirl were able to observe clearly – all too clearly – what happened next.

A family of black-and-white bear-like creatures, two adults and three cubs, came hurrying into the clearing. They were obviously terrified. They were also, obviously, the prey that the people with rifles were pursuing.

'What are those?' said Jax.

'Weren't you paying attention in your Historical Zoology lessons?' replied Flygirl. 'They're pandas.'

Jax did pay attention in his Historical Zoology lessons, but only when the animals he was learning about were predators or creepy-crawlies. That was why he had been able to identify Glote's NetShark phace as a great white, but had not recognized the pandas. 'Extinct?' he said.

Flygirl nodded solemnly. 'This is very bad. Hunting simulations are forbidden under UN Web regulations.'

'Maybe in the Web they are,' said Jax, 'but we're in the Net now.'

The panda cubs, squealing and trembling, huddled together in the middle of the clearing. Their parents prowled around them, urging them with prods and nudges to keep going. But it was no use. The cubs were exhausted and could not go another step.

The hunters closed in. Their shouts rose to a pitch of terrible, bloodthirsty intensity as they burst into the clearing. Halting, they raised their rifles and took aim at the defenceless pandas.

The adult pandas, hoping to protect their brood, placed themselves between the cubs and the hunters.

Flygirl averted her eyes. Jax would have looked away also, but he was both too appalled and too fascinated. He seemed incapable of moving his head.

The rifle shots were shockingly loud and seemed to go on forever. Mercifully, the din of the rifles drowned out the pandas' howls of pain.

When it was over, the clearing was filled with a drifting mist of gunsmoke. Jax was just about able to make out the bodies of the pandas lying in a heap on the ground. The adults had not been able to protect the cubs. All five of the pandas were dead.

Jax looked at the hunters' faces. Their eyes were huge and bright, and their grins were savagely wide. They whooped and yelped triumphantly, and high-fived one another.

Finally, Flygirl forced herself to look, too. What she saw filled her with disgust and outrage.

She had been responsible for the death of the guard hyena, a real animal in Realworld, and she felt bad about that but at least it had been an accident. She hadn't *intended* to kill the hyena, whereas these hunters had pursued the pandas for no other reason than to massacre them in cold blood. Admittedly, the pandas were only phaces but their wounds looked realistic – realistic enough to satisfy the hunters' horrible appetite for slaughter.

Incensed, Flygirl rose to her feet. 'Hey!' she shouted down to the hunters, and then, louder, 'HEY!'

The hunters turned and looked up at her, squinting and shading their eyes.

Flygirl was about to deliver an impassioned speech, telling the hunters that what they were doing was horrible and wrong and that they should be ashamed of themselves. But she never got the chance.

One of the hunters said, 'Look. Human prey!'

Instantly, all the hunters raised their rifles and took aim at Flygirl and Jax.

CHAPTER SIX

CARNIVAL

Flygirl stood there, dumbfounded. This couldn't be happening. These people couldn't, surely, be about to shoot at her and Jax. That sort of thing simply didn't happen in the Web.

Then she remembered. Like Jax had said, they weren't in the Web. They were in the Net which was not regulated the way the Web was. To be precise, they were in Davy Jones's Locker, where who-knows-what was permitted.

One of the hunters fired. The bullet ricocheted off the rock, mere millimetres from Flygirl's toes.

She flinched and instinctively ducked for cover. So did Jax. In the shock of being shot at, both momentarily forgot that nothing they experienced while wearing Websuits could actually hurt or harm them. They scrambled back from the summit of the rock outcrop, just as the rest of the hunters joined in the shooting. Bullets whizzed, whumped and whanged into the rock, sending up sprays of stone chips and splinters. Bullets also whizzed, whumped and whanged over the children's heads.

'Let's get out of here!' Flygirl shouted to Jax above the racket of gun-reports and ricochets.

They reached for the scuttle buttons on their wristpads. They pressed the buttons and, in a singing blue flash, found themselves . . . not, as expected, back in Realworld, but in a smoky bar filled with people dressed in denim and black motorbike leathers. The men were almost all burly and bearded, and each sported at least a couple of tattoos. Many of the women, too, were tattooed, and all of them wore their hair big and back-combed. Everyone was drinking and shouting raucously, and there were fights going on in various different corners of the bar. The fighters were hitting one another with pool cues, beer glasses, chairs, even tables. Onlookers cheered them on, encouraging them to greater heights of viciousness and passing them weapons if they were empty-handed. The air was filled with grunts and roars, the sound of things breaking and smashing, and the insistent grinding throb of very loud rock music.

Jax and Flygirl stared at the scene in disbelief.

'Must have been a malfunction with our scuttle buttons,' said Flygirl. 'A misaligned set of coordinates. Let's try again.'

Just as she said this, a pair of rotund, muscular bikers came swaggering up. One of the bikers had a pair of Hell's Angel wings tattooed on his neck, the other had a patch on the sleeve of his leather jacket that showed a skull in a helmet, with *Born To Be Wild* written below it in Gothic script.

'Well, lookee here,' said the Hell's Angel, pointing a stubby finger at Jax and Flygirl. There was a crust of black dirt under his ragged fingernail. 'Fresh meat.'

The other biker chuckled throatily and smacked his right fist into his left palm. 'OK, shrimps,' he said. 'Put 'em up.'

Jax and Flygirl, without needing to consult each other, scuttled . . .

They found themselves on the deck of a large, rusting ship that was heaving across the surface of a cold grey ocean. Hissing sprays of icy sea water splashed over the ship's gunwales, soaking Jax and Flygirl and making them shiver. A freezing wind whipped into their faces. The sky was a mass of dark, forbidding cloud, split here and there with flickering crackles of bright-blue lightning.

'What the heck's going on?' yelled Jax, grimacing with the cold. 'We're supposed to be home!'

'I don't know,' Flygirl yelled back. 'Something's wrong with our scuttle buttons, that's all I know.'

People in fluorescent-orange waterproofs and sou' wester hats were standing in a huddle at the ship's bows. They were looking out to sea, pointing and jabbering excitedly. The waterproofs were so big and heavy, it was hard to tell which of the people were men and which were women.

Jax and Flygirl craned their necks to see what the people were looking at.

Roughly half a kilometre ahead there was a pod of whales, swimming. There were at least a dozen of them, and they moved with a magnificent stately grace, their great barnacled grey backs arching slowly up from the water and then down again, their massive tails following, each one striking the waves with an almighty slap and splash. As each whale broke the surface, it shot a plume of white water from its blowhole fifteen metres into the air. It was an enthralling sight.

'This isn't so bad,' said Jax. 'Those people are just here to watch the whales.'

'I don't think so,' said Flygirl. 'Look.'

One of the people in waterproofs had stepped up onto a platform mounted on the ship's prow. Across his back, in large black letters, was the word 'SPECKTIONEER'.

On top of the platform sat a large object covered in a tarpaulin. The specktioneer pulled off the tarpaulin to reveal a harpoon gun.

The people at the bows looked on avidly as the speck-tioneer grasped the controls of the harpoon gun, took aim at the whales, and fired.

The harpoon shot from the gun with a loud percussive

whoosh! and went hurtling towards the whales, trailing a line of cable behind it.

The harpoon struck one of the whales in the back, and its explosive tip detonated.

The whale went under and came up again, and this time the water that spurted from its blowholes was pink.

'That's it!' said Flygirl angrily. 'I've had enough of this. Our scuttle buttons may not work, but there's nothing to stop me pulling my Websuit hood off.'

'Let's give the buttons one more try,' said Jax.

'All right,' she said, reluctantly. 'One more.'

They scuttled . . . and found themselves in a carnival. All around them were brightly-coloured tents, sideshows, fairground rides and stalls. Calliope music parped and oompah-pahed merrily. The sky was rippling blue again, but other than that, everything about the scene seemed pleasant and normal.

'Well, no one seems to be killing anything here,' said Flygirl. 'That's *something* at least. So, before we bat out for good, let's decide what we're going to do.'

'What do you mean?' said Jax.

'Well, we have to tell the Webcops what we've seen here,' Flygirl said, spelling it out as if it was the most obvious thing in the world. 'About the hunting zones, and about that biker bar.'

'The biker bar? What was illegal about that? It was just a combat zone, wasn't it? Plenty of those in the Web.'

'Combat zones are meant to be fantasy-based,' Flygirl explained. 'You know, you fight aliens or dragons, that sort of thing. Hitting other human beings in a realistic setting isn't allowed.'

'Oh,' said Jax. 'I see. But will the Webcops be able to do anything? After all, they're *Web*cops, not *Net*cops. Technically, they don't have any say over how the Net is run.'

'Not right now they don't, no.' Flygirl knew that the UN

was currently debating whether to extend the Webcops' powers to cover the Net as well as the Web. It was likely that the UN *would* pass a law giving the Webcops jurisdiction over the Net, but the decision would not be forthcoming for several months, and perhaps not even for a couple of years. Lawmaking was a slow, time-consuming process. 'But if someone told them what was going on here,' she continued, 'I think they'd find a way of shutting the Net down. Or, at any rate, shutting this part of it down.'

Jax nodded slowly. 'All right. I take your point. We'll go to the Webcops.'

Just then, to their left, a pair of women emerged from a tent, laughing. Usually laugher is a pleasant sound, but not in this instance. The laughter of these women had a hard, mocking edge to it.

'Did you get a load of *her*!' said one of them, shaking her head in disbelief.

'There was an awful lot to get a load of,' replied the other. 'Talk about a weight problem. She had a weight *crisis*!'

Flygirl glanced up at the sign above the tent entrance. It said:

Inside – Larger Than Life!
Three-Ton Tess!
The Fattest Lady in the World!
Ten Men to Her Hug Her –
A Freight Train to Lug Her!

'What a porker!' said the first woman. 'Oink oink!'

Her friend joined in. They strolled away, oinking merrily to each other.

The women's avatars were slim and well-proportioned, but Flygirl suspected that, in Realworld, both of them were somewhat on the portly side. Making fun of someone even larger than they were made them feel better about their own size.

She examined the signs on some of the other tents. One said:

Bonzo, the Dog-faced Boy!
He Fetches! He Begs! He Rolls Over and Plays Dead!

Accompanying the words was a picture showing a boy with a face so hairy and ugly that it did, indeed, resemble a dog's.

Another sign showed a picture of a man with the worst case of acne Flygirl had ever seen. There wasn't a square centimetre of his body that didn't have at least one large, flaring, yellow-headed spot on it. Even his eyelids and the palms of his hands were affected.

The sign said:

Zit-Man, The Living Pustule!
Unbelievable!
New Spots Will Appear Before Your Very Eyes!

Other tents showcased more people who, by virtue of some physical deformity or other, could be considered disgusting or freakish. There was a bearded lady, a man so thin he looked like a walking skeleton, a girl with scaly skin like an alligator's, and a host of midgets and pinheads and dwarves. All had been put on display so that Net users could come and have a shudder and a laugh at their expense.

The Webcops, thought Flygirl, are definitely going to hear about *this*.

She turned to say as much to Jax, only to discover that he was no longer by her side.

She looked around and caught sight of him entering a nearby tent, accompanied by a man who was dressed in a striped waistcoat and brown Derby hat.

Frowning, she set off after Jax.

*

While Flygirl had been busy gazing at the sideshow tents, Jax had heard someone calling out to him. 'Psst! Hey! Jax!'

Jax had turned around and pointed to himself quizzically, and a carnival barker had said, 'Yeah, you. I wanna word with you. C'mon over here.'

The barker, like the great white in the Building Blocks level bore a more-than-passing resemblance to a certain ponytailed computer genius of Jax's acquaintance. Older, and puffier around the cheeks and chin, but still unmistakably J Edgar Glote.

Curious, Jax went over to him.

'You look like a young fella with a lotta stuff weighing on his mind,' the barker said. He gestured at the large tent behind him. 'And I know a place where you can unburden yourself. Step inside and I'll show ya how.'

The barker held aside one of the tent-flaps. From inside the tent Jax heard the sound of gunfire.

Tentatively, he ventured in.

It was a shooting gallery of some sort. There was a row of wooden booths, and in each one there was a person taking potshots at a target. From where he was standing Jax couldn't see what the targets were. The people were all wearing large plastic headphones, presumably to protect their ears from the sound of the gunshots.

The barker took Jax by the shoulder and led him along the row. 'This is where folks can get their own back on people they don't like,' he said. He pointed to one man as they passed him. 'This fella's boss didn't give him the pay rise he deserves.' He pointed to a woman. 'This lady's husband has been ignoring her for several months, treating her like she wasn't there.' He pointed to a teenage boy, perhaps five years older than Jax. 'This young fella's been getting hassle from his parents, wanting to know when he's going to get a job and start making something of his life.'

He gestured along the entire row with a sweep of his arm. 'All of 'em have a grudge or a grievance against somebody. But instead of getting mad, they're getting even.'

The barker and Jax arrived at a vacant booth. The barker picked up the rifle that was lying on the shelf in the booth. It was similar to the rifles Jax had seen the panda-hunters carrying. It had a telescopic sight on top, and it looked powerful.

The barker handed the gun to Jax.

'Unlimited ammunition,' he said. 'Just aim and fire.'

Now, at last, Jax had a clear view of what everyone was shooting at. The targets were not concentric circles or tin ducks or little stars on pieces of paper. The targets were human figures, somewhat like mannequins, each suspended by chains from a scaffold frame. The figures were blank and featureless, except for their faces, which were fully detailed and realistic. Whenever a bullet found its mark, the figure that was hit would writhe as though in agony, its face contorting into a mask of pain and its mouth gaping in a soundless scream.

'The faces are 3D composites,' the barker informed him. 'We matte them in from identification photographs that are stored in various databases all over the world – banks, vehicle-licence offices, that kinda thing. Whoever's face you want, we can find it for you and put it on one of those figures. The screams are transmitted through the headphones. We thought it'd be better that way. Wouldn't want to alarm the folks outside, eh?'

Jax peered at the figure at the end of his aisle of the shooting gallery.

'There's already a face on my one,' he said.

'Sure there is,' said the barker. 'I kinda had a hunch you'd be coming, so I got one all ready just for you.'

'Who is it?' Jax asked, squinting.

'Take a look through the rifle sight.'

Jax held the rifle up to his eye, peered through its telescopic sight, and began adjusting the focus dial. Meanwhile the barker took a pair of headphones and slipped them on over Jax's head.

Muffled through the headphones, Jax heard the barker say, 'It's the guy who never has any time for you. The guy who's too wrapped up in himself to give you the attention you deserve. The guy who lets you have everything you want, except the one thing you really want – affection.'

Jax brought the figure's face into focus.

It was his father.

CHAPTER SEVEN

ROUSTABOUTS

'Go on,' said the barker to Jax. 'You know you want to. And it ain't really your father, only a digital representation of him. It'll scream like him and it'll kick and dance like it's in genuine pain – but it ain't really him. That's the wonder of it. You can get your own back without any comeback, because he'll never find out, never know. It's perfect, kid. Completely perfect.'

Jax stared through the telescopic sight at the image of his father's face. His father's face stared back, calm and impassive.

It wouldn't hurt, thought Jax. It might even feel quite good.

'Think about the fishing trip,' said the barker. 'Think about how many times he's said, "Maybe later, son." Too busy to bother, that's the truth of it. He made you a promise, you've tried to hold him to it, and he keeps wriggling out of it again and again. *Because he never meant to take you fishing at all, kid.* It was just something he said one day on the spur of the moment, hoping you'd forget about it. And to my mind, there ain't nothing worse than an idle promise.'

Jax's finger curled around the rifle trigger. He steadied the gun's butt against his shoulder, taking careful aim. The rifle felt right in his arms; felt natural.

'Nothing worse at all,' said the barker.

'Jax!'

Jax turned. Flygirl was standing just behind the barker. She had heard everything that had been said.

'Put the rifle down,' she said.

'Butt out, girlie,' growled the barker. 'This ain't got nothing to do with you.'

'This has everything to do with me,' replied Flygirl firmly. 'Jax is my friend, and you're trying to corrupt him. You're trying to make him like everyone else here in Davy Jones's Locker. You want him to be cruel, to do things without listening to his conscience.'

'Reckon you think you're pretty smart, dontcha, girlie?' sneered the barker. 'Smart and oh so worldly-wise. Well, for your information, what we do here isn't *corrupt* people. What we do is give them an outlet for their negative emotions. They can get things off their chests here, they can even up old scores, they can work out their problems and frustrations, and return to Realworld afterwards all the better for it. Calmer, more balanced, saner citizens. And that, if you ask me, ain't a bad thing at all.'

'No, it isn't a bad thing,' said Flygirl, 'it's a *terrible* thing. You're letting people do as they please without worrying about the consequences. That just encourages irresponsibility, both here and in Realworld.'

'If you say so, girlie,' said the barker with a patronizing smile. 'But you're wrong.'

'Don't call me *girlie*,' said Flygirl icily. She reached for Jax's hand. 'Come on, Jax. We're off.'

Jax glanced back at the figure with his father's face. Did he really want to see and hear his father scream?

No. No, he didn't.

He might resent his father sometimes, but he didn't *hate* him.

He lowered the rifle and removed the headphones. He set both items down on the shelf in front of him.

Flygirl, who was still holding on to his arm, gave him a reassuring squeeze. 'Well done,' she said.

'No, not well done,' said the barker. 'Big mistake.' He put two fingers in his mouth and blew a shrill, piercing whistle. 'Hey, Rube!' he yelled.

Two men wearing checked shirts and flat caps entered through the tent-flap. They were broad-shouldered and barrel-chested, with faces like baked potatoes and fists like cooked hams.

In the days when real carnivals toured America, men like these were known as roustabouts. They were the ones who erected and dismantled the tents and sideshows, and carried out all the other manual tasks relating to the carnival. These two, however, looked as if their particular speciality was mangling, or perhaps crushing, or maybe pounding – one of those, certainly, and probably all three.

'These kids,' said the barker, indicating Jax and Flygirl, 'don't seem to appreciate the delights we got on offer.'

'Ain't *dat* a shame,' said one of the roustabouts.

'Real pity,' said the other.

They began moving menacingly towards Flygirl and Jax.

'Run!' said Flygirl.

Jax didn't need any further prompting. Together, they turned and ran. The roustabouts set off after them at a lumbering pace.

Jax and Flygirl sprinted along the row of booths. The roustabouts followed, two hulking great masses of meat and muscle. The people using the shooting gallery were so intent on inflicting pain on their enemies that they were oblivious to the drama behind them.

Jax reached the end of the shooting gallery first, several metres ahead of Flygirl, who was hampered by the unresponsiveness of Lioness's Websuit but was still, fortunately, quicker on her feet than the roustabouts.

Turning, Jax saw that there was nowhere to go. The only

way in and out of the tent was by the flap through which he and Flygirl had entered. The pair of roustabouts were between them and it, and were gaining on them rapidly.

As Flygirl caught up with him, she reached down and pulled up the bottom edge of the tent, creating a gap between it and the ground. The gap was just large enough for them to squeeze through.

'Quickly!' she said.

Obediently, Jax got down on his hands and knees and wriggled through the gap. Standing up on the other side, he had a moment to register that he was in a narrow alley between two rows of tents before he grabbed the edge of the shooting-gallery tent from Flygirl and held it up for her.

The two roustabouts were almost upon her as she threw herself flat on the ground and thrust herself headfirst into the gap.

She was almost through when she felt a powerful hand grab her left ankle. She grunted and kicked at the hand with her right foot. Her heel connected with the roustabout's knuckles. He yelled and cursed but he did not let go.

'Jax!' said Flygirl as she felt herself being hauled back inside the tent. 'Grab my wrists!'

Jax pulled hard at Flygirl until her entire torso was dragged clear of the tent, but her legs remained inside.

The second roustabout seized Flygirl's other ankle, and together the two men tugged her back until only her head, shoulders and arms were outside the tent.

Jax dug his heels in and pulled with all his might. Flygirl slid forwards until she was half in, half out of the tent again.

It would have been comical if it hadn't been deadly serious – Flygirl being used as the rope in a desperate tug-of-war. She certainly failed to see the funny side of it.

'Come on, Jax, for heaven's sake!' she cried. 'Put your back into it! Pull!'

Jax bent over and braced himself for one last effort. At the same time, Flygirl started kicking her legs in the air like a swimmer, making it difficult for the roustabouts to maintain a proper grip on her. Jax's feet trowelled twin gouges in the grass as he heaved at his friend. Flygirl's waist emerged, then her bottom, her thighs, her calves, and finally her feet, still with the roustabouts' hands clasping her ankles.

Jax let go of her wrists and, before the roustabouts had a chance to drag her back, he stamped on their hands one after another in quick succession.

The roustabouts yelped and snatched back their hands, uttering a stream of oaths.

Flygirl scrambled to her feet and dusted herself down. 'Thanks, Jax,' she said. 'I owe you one.'

'No, you don't,' said Jax. 'You stopped me doing something in there that I would probably have regretted forever. We're even.'

They smiled at each other.

'Hoods off, then?' said Flygirl, miming the action of removing a Websuit hood.

'Hey, Rube!'

The barker was standing at the end of the alley of tents. Three more of the roustabouts were with him. He pointed at Jax and Flygirl. 'Get 'em, boys!' he ordered.

The roustabouts lurched down the alley. Jax and Flygirl had no choice but to start running again.

The tents were lined up so closely together that their guy-ropes overlapped. Jax and Flygirl were forced to hurdle the guy-ropes one after another, which slowed them down. Luckily, the ropes slowed the roustabouts down even more. The roustabout who was leading the pack tripped on one of them and fell flat on his face, and the two following him, being phaces of limited mip-capacity, stumbled right over him.

Jax and Flygirl watched as one after another, like man-sized dominoes, the roustabouts went crashing to the ground. All three of them tried to get up at once with the result that none of them actually managed it. They all fell flailing to the ground again. One of them became so snarled up in the guy-ropes that when they all tried to rise a second time, the result was similarly disastrous. The three roustabouts writhed and cursed on the ground, calling one another rude names and struggling, without success, to pull themselves upright and resume the chase.

'Better keep going,' Flygirl prompted Jax.

They turned only to find their way was blocked by a peculiar-looking man.

He had coffee-coloured skin, a goatee beard, a long, aquiline nose, and limpid brown eyes, and he was dressed in white tie and tails. This might seem normal enough, but he also had a red silk turban on his head that was crowned with a long white feather. Not only that, but set into the middle of his forehead there was a large, sparkling ruby, and on his shoulder there perched a soot-black rook.

The man appeared to be Indian in origin, but his voice was like nothing Jax or Flygirl had heard before. It buzzed and flitted up and down through each word he spoke, like a bee uncertain where to alight.

'coMe wITh mE,' he said. 'i caN HeLP yOu.'

CHAPTER EIGHT

SWAMI

Both Jax and Flygirl took a wary step backwards.

'pLeaSe,' said the man. 'I CaN shOw You tHE wAy oUT of hErE.'

'How can we be sure you aren't with *them*?' Flygirl gestured over her shoulder at the tangle of roustabouts who were still struggling to get to their feet.

The strange man gave a sly smile. 'AlLOW me tO pRoVe It tO yOu. stEp AsIde.'

Jax and Flygirl cautiously did as he had asked.

The man raised his hand to his shoulder and let the rook step onto his index finger. As he brought his hand down, the rook flapped its wings to maintain its balance, cawing croakily.

Holding the rook in front of him, the man said the following words – an incantation, of sorts:

ROOK
ROCK
RACK
RANK
DANK
DARK
DARE
DIRE
DIVE
DOVE

Then he gave the bird a deft, double-handed twist, apparently turning it inside-out.

All of a sudden he was no longer holding a cawing black rook. He was holding a cooing white dove.

At the exact same instant that the rook changed into a dove, the three roustabouts disappeared in a big explosion and a puff of smoke.

When the smoke cleared, in their place were three white rabbits.

The rabbits looked perplexed for a moment, but then set about doing what rabbits do: hopping around, nibbling the grass and twitching their noses.

'Venomous,' said Jax. 'How did you do that?'

'THEre iS A sAyIng, iS thERe nOt? "a gOoD mAGicIaN NevEr REvEalS hIs seCreTS."'

'Is that what you are?' said Flygirl. 'A magician?'

'I pREfeR tO cAIL MyseLf A SwAMI,' said the man, placing the dove on his shoulder. 'iT Is a MOrE eXoTic aPpelLaTioN, aNd i Am, wIThoUt a doUBt, EXceEdIngLy exoTIc. nOw, COme. WE MuSt hIDE. OThERs wIll bE lOokInG For YoU.'

The Swami led them along the alley, stepping over the guy-ropes. Soon they came to the back of a tent that was decked out in an Eastern style, with ornate trimming around its edges and hypnotically swirly patterns picked out in gold on its canvas.

The Swami traced a fingertip over some of the patterns, and an oval opening appeared in the tent canvas.

He stepped through the opening and invited Jax and Flygirl to follow him.

They exchanged glances.

'Well?' said Jax out of the side of his mouth.

'I think we can trust him,' said Flygirl, although she didn't sound entirely convinced. 'But if he tries anything funny, we do a bat, OK?'

Jax nodded, and they entered the tent.

The opening sealed itself silently behind them.

The tent was small and dimly lit by candles. It was filled with a stage magician's props and paraphernalia: wands, top hats, boxes decorated with stars and crescent moons, sets of steel rings linked together, tall cabinets large enough to hold (and hide) a human being, dozens of packs of oversized playing cards, and lots of other items. Everything looked new and unused, as if it was all just there for show.

The Swami pulled out two chairs and invited the children to sit on them.

'YOu hAve hAD TroUbLe lEAvIng, hAVe yOU NoT?' he said.

'Our scuttle buttons are down the plug,' replied Flygirl. 'Instead of taking us back to Realworld, they've been transporting us from one zone of Davy Jones's Locker to another.'

'maY i INSpEct?'

Flygirl extended her left arm, and the Swami grasped her wristpad and peered hard at it for several seconds. At the same time, Flygirl surreptitiously touched the control knob on the frame of her dark glasses and peered hard at *him*.

'AH, yeS,' he said. 'It aPpEArS THaT SoMeoNE hAs BeEn tAMpErInG wITH yOur SOfTwAre. a virUs HaS beeN iNtrOdUCed.'

'That's not possible,' said Jax. 'Our realoes get regular booster inoculations.'

'nONeTheLEsS,' said the Swami.

'The octopuses!' said Flygirl, with a snap of her fingers. 'It must have been them. They were wrapped around our wristpads for a while. They could easily have passed on a contact virus.'

'Can you get rid of the virus so we can get back home?' Jax asked the Swami.

'BuT Of cOURrSe,' said the Swami, with a small, polite bow. 'hOlD sTiLL,' he told Flygirl.

He leaned over her wristpad and began staring at it with a concentrated frown. A finger-thick beam of red light erupted from the ruby embedded in his forehead, bathing Flygirl's wristpad in a crimson glow.

Slowly, lugubriously, something gelatinous and green started oozing up from beneath her scuttle button. The gelatinous green thing wormed its way out as though the light from the Swami's ruby was making life so uncomfortable for it inside the wristpad that it was forced out into the open.

When the green thing had emerged completely, the beam of red light shut itself off.

'tHerE iS yOUr VIruS,' said the Swami, plucking the gelatinous green thing from Flygirl's wristpad. He held it up between thumb and forefinger. It squirmed and writhed stickily. It looked like a cross between a slug and a lump of phlegm.

The Swami frowned again, and another beam of light shot from his ruby, this one as narrow and focused as a laser beam. The virus, caught in the beam, began bubbling and sizzling like a sausage under a grill. In no time at all, it had shrivelled up to a charred lump of dead matter.

The Swami tossed it aside and repeated the whole process with Jax's wristpad.

'dONe,' he said, flinging aside a second cooked virus. 'NoW You mAy leAvE WhEn yOU sO DesIre.'

'Thank you,' said Flygirl.

'A plEaSurE,' said the Swami, bowing again. 'bUT fIrST, PLeAsE lIstEN tO ME. i HaVe BEen MonItorInG tHiS pLaCE foR SoME tiMe. IT iS nOT a GooD PLaCE to Be, EsPecIalLY fOr cHiLdRen.'

'We know,' said Flygirl, with feeling. 'And we intend to do something about it.'

'tHAt Is goOd.'

'Who *are* you?' said Jax. 'Are you a phace? An undercover Webcop?'

'i,' said the Swami, 'aM aN ObSeRVer. mY dUTiEs ArE TO rEconNOiTrE aND REPorT BAcK.'

'Like a scout,' said Flygirl.

'pREciSeLy.'

'But who for?'

'IT iS AgainSt My ORDeRs To tEll YOU. aLl wiLL bE REVeALeD in TimE. It Is ALSo AGAinSt mY ordErs tO INTeRFerE wiTH whATevEr i Am obsERvIng.'

'But you've done that already,' Jax pointed out. 'You saved us from those three men, and you got rid of the virus.'

The Swami acknowledged this with a resigned nod. 'I fElT oblIgeD tO hElp. i cOUld nOT MerELy stANd bY aND dO noThING. And SinCE I hAVe disOBeYed onE oRDer, I fEeL lESs rEluCTaNT abOut dISoBEyiNG ANOthEr. i WISh tO hELp yOu FURthER.'

'That's very kind of you,' said Flygirl, 'but I'm not sure what you can do.'

'yOu sAW, wiTH thOse thREe mEn, hoW I ReNDeRED tHE harMfuL HaRMLesS.'

'With that dove,' said Jax.

The Swami nodded. He took the dove down and held it out to Jax.

'TaKE It,' he said. 'AnD RemeMBeR tHIS. eveRyTHInG conTainNS, inSiDE iT, elemENtS Of ITS oPPosIte. GoOD AnD bad, negATIvE anD POsItiVE, blaCk And WhitE – WHerEvEr yOU fiND tHE onE, yOU WiLL NEceSsArilY FinD ThE oTher. thUs iT Is eAsIEr thAn yoU Might tHinK tO trANsFORM ThE onE iNTo thE oThEr.'

Jax hesitated before accepting the dove from the Swami. He wasn't sure what possible use the bird could be to him.

It was almost as if the Swami had read his mind. 'wHEn

tHE TimE COMeS,' he said, with a slow, enigmatic blink, 'yOU wiLl knOW whAT tO Do.'

From outside there came the sound of several men shouting at once. The children recognized, among the voices, the voice of the barker.

'gO,' said the Swami. 'IF TheY enTer hERe, I wIlL teLL ThEM i hAVe NoT seeN You.'

'Thank you,' Flygirl said to the Swami. To Jax she said, 'You and I had better talk again soon.'

They hit their scuttle buttons.

Jax yanked off the hood of his Websuit and took a long, deep breath of air. Familiar air. The air of his Webroom.

His father was standing in front of him, holding the Net junction-box, which was still plugged into his Websuit.

Larry Hamlyn did not look happy.

CHAPTER NINE

DEAL?

As he angrily unplugged the Net junction-box from Jax's Websuit, Larry Hamlyn said to his son, 'I don't make too many demands on you, Jerry. In fact, I let you do pretty much as you please. And yet, the one time I do instruct you specifically not to do something, what happens? You disobey me.'

Jax tried to protest, but his father would not listen.

'I don't want to hear it,' said Hamlyn, holding up his hand like a policeman stopping traffic. 'Whatever you've got to say, whatever excuse you have – I don't want to hear it. I don't even want to know where *this* came from.' He shook the junction-box. 'The Days home-shopping site, I'll bet. Well, I hope it's under guarantee, because I'm sending it back there first thing tomorrow.'

'But—'

'No, Jerry! This isn't something you can talk your way out of. I was serious when I told you I didn't want you batting into the Net, and I'm serious now when I say that you've let me down badly.'

'I know, Dad,' said Jax, and he tried to explain where the junction-box had really come from and then tell his father about Davy Jones's Locker and the things he and Flygirl had seen and experienced there. But again, Hamlyn cut him off.

'Not another word, Jerry. I'm taking this box and locking

it away in my study where you won't be able to get to it –
and *you* are going to your bedroom to sit and think about
what you've done.'

That, for Jax, was the final straw. If his father didn't want
to know what was going on inside the Net, then fine. He
could learn about it from the Webcops.

Glaring at his father, Jax shrugged out of his Websuit,
letting it fall in a crumpled heap around his ankles. Then he
strode out of the Webroom without so much as a backward
glance.

He had dinner that evening alone in his bedroom. A tray-
drone brought him the meal on its back. After dinner, he
played listlessly for a while with his PseudoPup, which got
up to all sorts of mischievous pranks in a vain attempt to
cheer him up. Then he turned on the TV and climbed into
bed to watch. Normally television was a poor substitute for
the intense virtual adventures he could have in his Websuit, but tonight, after his experiences in Davy Jones's
Locker, it was a reassuringly two-dimensional and non-
threatening source of entertainment. He channel-surfed
until he grew too tired to operate the remote control. Soon
he had fallen asleep, the TV set switching itself off
automatically the moment his eyelids closed.

The following morning, Jax woke, got up, and went to
the kitchen to make himself some breakfast. He was hoping
his father would be there. In the light of a new day, his
father's temper might have cooled. He might be in a
calmer, more receptive frame of mind and might be willing
to listen to what Jax had to tell him.

But his father was not there. Instead, sitting at the
breakfast bar, sipping a cup of coffee and looking very
much at home, thank you, was J Edgar Glote.

'Hiya, kiddo!' said Glote. 'How's it hanging?'

'Where's my dad?' Jax asked.

'Been and gone,' replied Glote. 'Meeting with his accountant, I think he said. Told me, if I saw you, to pass on a message. He's got a charity fund-raiser to attend this afternoon, so he won't be home for lunch, but this evening you and he are going to have a good long talk.'

'A charity fund-raiser? In the afternoon? That doesn't sound right.'

'Ah, you know these charity people – they'll ask for their handouts at any time of day,' said Glote with a sneer. 'Stop me if I'm being nosy here, Jerry, but from the way your father was talking, I got the distinct impression that you and he still haven't patched up your differences.'

Jax said nothing. He programmed the kitchen's pancake-maker to prepare him six wheat pancakes with maple syrup.

'You know what you guys' trouble is?' said Glote. Without waiting for a response from Jax, he went on. 'You're both as obstinate as each other. It must be a hereditary thing. Like father, like son. Neither of you's prepared to back down when you have an argument. Neither of you'll concede so much as a millimetre of ground. So you go around mad at each other all the time and nothing gets resolved.'

'Thank you for that penetrating insight,' said Jax sarcastically.

'Hey, you're welcome.'

The pancake-maker pinged, and Jax opened its hatch and took out a plate stacked with steaming, syrup-drenched pancakes. He carried the plate to the breakfast bar and set to work on its contents with a fork.

Glote watched him eat for a while, and then said, 'So how was it?'

'How was what?' said Jax through a mouthful of pancake.

'The Net.'

Jax phrased his answer carefully. 'It was . . . different.'

'Did you like Davy Jones's Locker?'

Jax laid down his fork. 'I had a few problems there.'

'Problems with your scuttle button?'

'Yeah.' Then Jax frowned. 'How did you know that?'

'Think about it, kid.'

Slowly it dawned on Jax. '*You* did it. *You* were responsible for the virus.'

'Give the boy a medal!' said Glote, chuckling.

'But why? Why did you want me not to bat out?'

'I didn't want you not to bat out, exactly. I wanted you to have the opportunity to experience all the different environments that Davy Jones's Locker has to offer, and I figured installing an anti-scuttle virus in the passcode was the best way to do that. As you no doubt discovered, there was a limit on the virus. Six presses on your scuttle button, and you were back in Realworld. I figured six zones would be enough to give you a good sample of the range of experiences available. So, what did you think? How was the whaling-ship scenario? And the seal-culling? And the Deep South plantation zone?'

Jax thought it best not to mention that, thanks to the Swami, he had not had to visit those last two zones.

'It was horrible,' he said. 'All the killing, the violence—'

'Yeah, but deep down, in your heart of hearts, didn't you find it just the teensiest bit thrilling, too?' said Glote. 'You see, Jerry, Davy Jones's Locker is a place where people can do as they please. That's the glory of it. It's a place where no one – not the Webcops, and especially not a father who ignores you most of the time – can tell you what to do. It's everyone's *dream*. A world without rules, restrictions, responsibilities.'

'Is that what the sales realoes at the brochure site mean when they talk about utopias?' Jax asked, remembering what Lioness had said in Loreland the other day.

'You could look at it that way, I guess. The word *utopia* is used as a kind of test for prospective subscribers. If a subscriber reacts in a certain way to it, gives certain specific reactions, that tells us that he or she may be the sort of person who would enjoy Davy Jones's Locker. Then one of the NetSharks will approach him or her in the Net and make an offer. There's a surcharge for using Davy Jones's Locker, but people don't mind paying it at all, once they've had a taste of the place.'

'And you've kept all this from my dad?'

'More easily than you'd think, Jerry. Your father's no fool, but he's only a money-man, an investor. He owns Mesh Inc., but I'm the one who actually runs the company. Besides, Davy Jones's Locker is kind of a shared secret. The only people who know about it are the Netware programmers who created it and the Net-subscribers who use it, and they all realize that in order for it to continue to exist, they mustn't tell anyone else about it.'

'So why are you telling *me*?' Jax asked.

'Isn't it obvious? Jerry, pal, I want to go into partnership with you.'

Jax paused a moment to let this sink in. 'What, like a business deal?'

'Not quite so formal. More a kind of *friends* thing. See, Jerry, your dad's investment is crucial to the Net and to Mesh Inc. I won't bore you with all the complicated financial stuff. Suffice to say that we're showing a profit, but if your dad were to pull out his money for whatever reason, the company'd go under. Glug glug glug. That would be bad at any time, but particularly now, because I'm right in the middle of delicate negotiations with several Pacific Rim nations to market and distribute Netware there. It's a multimillion-dollar deal, and if anything were to mess it up, I'd get pretty mad.'

Jax had the feeling that he didn't want to be around if Glote ever got mad. Glote acted all nice and friendly on the surface, but Jax sensed there was a simmering bad temper beneath, like the molten core of an apparently-dormant volcano, ready to boil over at the slightest provocation.

'And you want me on your side,' said Jax. 'That's what this is all about.'

'Exactamundo, Jerry, my boy! I want you on my side. I want you batting on my team, as it were.'

'In case my dad tries to pull his money out. You think I could talk him out of it, if necessary.'

'If you couldn't, who could?' said Glote, with a simple shrug.

'But why? Why would I want to help you?'

' 'Cause you liked it in Davy Jones's Locker, Jerry. I know what you said – how it was horrible and all that. That's what you said with your *lips*, but your *eyes* told me a whole different story.'

Jax could not deny that there was some truth in this. In the shooting gallery he had been sorely tempted to put bullets into the mannequin with his father's face.

'And I'm thinking about the future as well,' Glote went on. 'After all . . .' He scratched the top of his head. 'What's a tactful way of putting this? Your dad, Jerry, isn't going to be around for ever, if you know what I mean. And when he's gone, who's going to inherit his wealth? His one and only son, of course.'

Jax thought about Flygirl. Evidently Glote was unaware that he had not visited Davy Jones's Locker alone. 'What if,' he said, choosing his words carefully, 'someone was to report what they'd seen in Davy Jones's Locker to the Webcops?'

'Jerry,' said Glote, shaking his head. 'Use your brain. The public associate the name of one person, and one person alone, with the Net – Larry Hamlyn. Hardly anyone's heard of J Edgar Glote, and I'm happy for it to stay that way. I'm not a limelight kind of guy. I like to remain behind the scenes, in the shadows. Your dad's the one everybody immediately thinks of whenever the Net is mentioned. So if there were any kind of scandal involving the Net, the blame would *appear* to lie squarely with your dad, never mind who was really responsible. Eminent people live by their reputations, and Larry Hamlyn's reputation would be in ruins.' Glote's eyes turned as cold and steely as the spectacle-rims that framed them. 'You bear that in mind, Jerry,' he said, and finished his coffee and stood up. 'And also bear in mind the offer I've made.'

As he left the kitchen, Glote said, 'So long, *partner.*'

A couple of minutes later Jax heard the sound of Glote starting his car outside and driving away. Staring at the half-eaten pancakes in front of him, he pondered deeply over everything Glote had said.

Jax came to the conclusion that he didn't have any choice. For his father's sake, he would have to keep quiet about Davy Jones's Locker. He would have to do this even though it meant that he was going to be stuck, for the rest of his life, in an uneasy alliance with J Edgar Glote.

He felt as if he had made a pact with the Devil.

Then a thought occurred to him. What if Flygirl had already contacted the Webcops?

He leaped to his feet and headed for the nearest video-phone in the house.

The N'Doubas' v-phone number was stored in the house CPU's dial-memory. At the press of a single button, Jax was put through.

Mrs N'Douba answered. She was a handsome woman, with glossy, curly black hair held back by a gold headband, and fine smile-wrinkles around her eyes.

'Jerry,' she said. 'How nice to see you. How are you?'

'OK, thanks, Mrs N'Douba. Is Flygirl home?'

'Is *who* home? Oh, you mean Anita.'

'Yeah, sorry. Anita.'

'You children and your alter-egos,' said Mrs N'Douba,

with a mildly despairing laugh. 'It's a whole different world. Yes, I believe she's in. I'll go and fetch her.'

A minute later, Flygirl's face appeared on the screen in front of Jax. On the rare occasions when Jax saw her without her dark glasses, such as now, it always took him a moment to adjust. She looked a completely different person. More approachable, less aloof and mysteriously wise.

'Flygirl,' he said, 'please tell me you haven't spoken to the Webcops yet.'

'Why?' she asked, with a hint of suspicion.

'Just tell me you haven't.'

'As a matter of fact I haven't.'

Relief surged through Jax.

'It was pretty late when I got back in last night,' Flygirl went on, 'and I thought that before we did anything we ought to agree on the best way of going about it. It's, what, just past eight a.m. where you are? I figured you'd only have just got up, so I was going to leave it till nine to call you. Give you a chance to suck some breakfast. So what's the problem, Jax? It sounds to me like you've changed your mind about telling the Webcops about Davy Jones's Locker.'

Jax explained to her why he didn't want the Webcops to know about Davy Jones's Locker. He also told her how Glote had sabotaged their scuttle buttons and then had offered him the prospect of a sort of partnership.

'You *have* to tell your father about Davy Jones's Locker,' said Flygirl, when Jax had finished. 'There's no alternative.'

'But then what? Dad would be forced to go to the Webcops, and then there'd be a huge scandal. Glote's right. Everyone would blame Larry Hamlyn, not him.'

'Why? Davy Jones's Locker wasn't your father's idea.'

'Yes, but that's not how it would look.'

'You've told me about this Glote person before. You've always said he gives you the creeps because he's so silky.'

'Well, he is.'

'So, why do you trust him now?'

'Because everything he's said sounds plausible.'

Flygirl sighed impatiently. 'Jax, haven't you learned anything from all those hours we've spent in Loreland? All the leprechauns and Rumplestiltskins and Snow Queens *sound* plausible, but you have to take everything they say with a pinch of salt.'

'That's the Web, Flygirl. This is Realworld. You know,' he added, viciously, 'sometimes you can be such a *phreak*.'

The comment clearly stung Flygirl, and he immediately regretted making it. He apologized. 'Sorry. That was a basement-level thing to say.'

'*Ziko ndaba*,' Flygirl replied, with a half-hearted smile.

There was an awkward silence. Then Jax said, 'If only there was some way we could stop everyone using Davy Jones's Locker and get the place shut down, but without involving the Webcops.'

'Well, there isn't, so we're just going to have to do as we originally planned,' said Flygirl adamantly. 'Inform the Webcops. And while we're doing that, we ought to tell them about that Swami character as well. I had a squint at his code while he was looking at my wristpad. I've never seen code like it on any phace or realoe ever. It was weird, complex stuff. The algorithms were all back-to-front, and I'd swear it wasn't in binary. Jax, your eyes have gone all faraway. Are you listening to me?'

'Hmm? Oh, sorry, Flygirl. Something you said's just given me an idea.'

Flygirl's eyes narrowed. 'I'm not sure I like the sound of this.'

'No, seriously. I think I know what we can do. And if we do it right, the Webcops needn't ever be involved.'

He outlined his idea to Flygirl. She said it was a crazy plan and had the square-root-of-zero chance of succeeding. He said it might work, with her help. She said that even with her help, it wouldn't work. He begged her to give it a try, at least, and if the plan failed, *then* they would go to the Webcops.

Eventually, reluctantly, Flygirl gave in and agreed to help him.

'Thanks, Flygirl. You're widow.'

'Flatterer. All right, so when do you want to put this harebrained scheme of yours into effect?'

'My dad's not going to be back till this evening,' said Jax. 'Now seems as good a time as any.'

CHAPTER TEN

INSIDE-OUT

What Jax had asked of Flygirl wasn't, in theory, impossible. It was just that no one had ever tried it before.

Websuited-up, she batted into the Web, then punched buttons on her wristpad, entering a code Jax had given her.

The period of blue-and-tone went on for considerably longer than normal. Then, all of a sudden, Flygirl felt herself being wrenched and wrung and strangely *stretched*, as though her body was a lump of pâté that someone was forcing, millimetre by squidgy millimetre, down a drinking straw.

There were moments of claustrophobic panic, when she thought she was going to suffocate, thought she was never going to draw breath again . . .

And then, millimetre by squidgy millimetre, she found herself expanding again, opening out and able to inhale and exhale normally.

She was still herself, but she was also something else.

She had many eyes now, each electronically remote on the end of a long fibre-optic stalk, and each able to zoom and pan and memorize.

She had many ears, too, which waited, ever-ready, to hear certain preset verbal commands.

She had skin of brick and metal and glass, and dozens of delicate inner organs that were attuned to the tiniest movements and changes in temperature in all of the many compartments inside her.

She had several noses that were particularly sensitive to smoke, so that, if she smelled any, she could instantly raise the alarm and send down showers of water from a sprinkler system to extinguish a fire.

She could even, after a fashion, taste. Wherever there was dirt or dust, it was almost as though she could feel it on her tongue, and she could send cleaning-drones to rid the site in question of all offensive, unwanted matter.

She had accessed the central processing unit of the Hamlyn residence in Los Angeles. Jax had made this possible by setting up a channel between the CPU and the Web via his spare Websuit's interface. She and the CPU were now intimately linked. Its physical sensations were hers – a bizarre feeling, though not an entirely unpleasant one. The house had software routines that were like simple, homely emotions. Flygirl felt the pride it took in efficiently supplying shelter and comfort to its occupants. She felt its sense of vigilance as, twenty-four hours a day, it looked after and over the man and the boy who lived in it. In a way the house was a mother to both Larry and Jerry Hamlyn. It protected and provided.

Quickly adjusting to her new reality, Flygirl located Jax through one of the house's indoor surveillance cameras. He was where he had said he would be, waiting outside the door to his father's study. She looked down at him from the corner of the corridor ceiling. She couldn't talk to him – the CPU was not equipped with a voice synthesizer – but she showed him that she had arrived in the CPU by overriding the lock-command that Jax's father had put on the door.

The door slid open. Jax threw a thank-you wave to the surveillance camera's lens and entered the study.

He searched the room high and low for the Net junction-

box, but it was in none of the drawers of his father's desk,
nor was it on any of the shelves.

'Open safe,' he said.

The phrase 'Open safe' spoken by anyone but Larry
Hamlyn automatically registered with the house CPU as
Voice-Pattern Mismatch. The CPU was programmed not to
respond unless Hamlyn himself uttered the command.

Flygirl overrode that programming.

In the study, one of the pair of Van Goghs swung away
from the wall on hinges. Behind was the door to a
reinforced ceramic safe.

Jax reached up and placed his right hand on the scanning
plate on the safe door. The scanning plate read his
palmprint and fingerprints and transmitted a second *Mismatch* signal to the CPU. The hand did not belong to Larry
Hamlyn. Similar, but not quite.

Again, Flygirl arranged for the mismatch to be disregarded. The safe door unlocked and opened.

The Net junction-box was inside.

Jax took it and headed for his Webroom. Flygirl, meanwhile, closed and re-locked both the safe door and the
study door.

For the time being, she couldn't do anything more for
her friend, except wish him luck.

And remember the words, Jax, she thought. Remember
the words.

Arriving at the Net's Building Blocks, Jax found the octopus
passcode was, as before, still attached to his arm. That was
good. If the octopus was there, it meant the anti-scuttle
virus was being reinstalled in his wristpad. The virus was
not crucial to his plan, but its presence would make things
simpler.

The octopus, when asked, dragged him down under
the Building Blocks to the coral outgrowth, and from

there they passed through into the algae-illuminated cavern, where the octopus opened the treasure chest for him.

Then he was in the jungle again. The octopus was gone, but the dove that the Swami had given him was there, perched on his shoulder. Jax stroked the top of its white head with one finger, and it closed its eyes and cooed pleasurably.

'You and I,' he said to the dove, 'have work to do.'

It wasn't long before he heard the cry and crash of hunters. He strode calmly in the direction of the sound, until he was able to see a group of khaki-clad figures moving between the trees. Ahead of them, a family of terrified pandas were fleeing as fast as they could, which, for such slow and docile animals, was not very fast.

Jax broke into a slow run, keeping pace with the pandas. As he ran, he took the dove from his shoulder and clasped it in both hands, the way the Swami had done.

Earlier, with Flygirl's help, he had pieced together the ten-word incantation the Swami had used. Now he repeated it aloud:

ROOK
ROCK
RACK
RANK
DANK
DARK
DARE
DIRE
DIVE
DOVE

At the same time, he copied the twisting action the Swami had used, bending the dove with both hands as though trying to push its belly up through its back.

The dove protested, flapping its wings and fluting shrilly.

Other than that, nothing happened. The hunters continued their pursuit, closing in on the pandas.

Jax stopped in his tracks. Why wasn't it working? Why
hadn't the hunters been transformed into rabbits or chip-
munks or mice or something equally small and harmless?

Then he realized why. In the order he had spoken them,
the words changed 'ROOK' to 'DOVE'. But the rook was
already a dove. He had to change it back.

Grasping the dove again, he repeated the words, but in
reverse order. With a certain amount of stumbling and
hesitation he got from 'DOVE' to 'ROOK'.

And as he said, 'ROOK,' he gave the bird a twist, and felt
it fold between his fingers as easily as a table napkin.

He looked down and saw that he had a croaking, coal-
black rook in his hands.

Then he looked up and saw that the hunters were still
hunters. As he watched, however, he saw their expressions
shift from bloodthirsty determination to panic and fear.
They turned on their heels and started running away from,
instead of after, the pandas.

The pandas were now the ones doing the chasing. No
longer were they rotund, cuddly, timid creatures. All of
them, including the cubs, had grown to three metres tall,
and long, sharp claws had sprung from their paws, and
rows of fearsome fangs filled their mouths. They had
morphed into monster-pandas, and they bellowed and
snarled terrifyingly as they loped after the hunters, as
intent on slaughtering the hunters as the hunters had been
on slaughtering them.

One by one the scared hunters dropped their rifles and
batted out. Their avatars became faint, blurry smears, as
though a giant hand had rubbed them sideways. Swiftly the
smears faded into invisibility.

Seeing this, Jax chuckled heartily to himself. The rook,
apparently sharing his amusement, let out a hoarse cackle.

'Next zone,' Jax said, and pressed his scuttle button.

The anti-scuttle virus did its thing. He was transported to the biker bar, where, it transpired, there was a huge brawl going on. One of the two-person fights had got out of control, and now everyone in the room, men and women alike, had become involved. Fists were flying. Hair was being pulled. Punches and kicks were landing left, right and centre. Knocked-out teeth were hurtling through the air.

In the midst of this rowdy free-for-all, Jax cupped the rook protectively to his chest and again went through the incantation, ROOK to DOVE.

As he twisted the bird, a sudden calm fell. All fighting in the bar ceased, and everyone looked at everyone else, blinking, and perplexed.

Every person in the room except Jax had sprouted a pair of huge white wings and a halo. Their leather and denim outfits had been replaced by flowing white robes. Those who had been holding weapons now found themselves holding harps.

There were no Hell's Angels in the bar any more. Only angels.

Jax hadn't expected this. He had turned the rook back into a dove simply so that he would be able to turn it back into a rook again. However, in the event, he couldn't have hoped for a better outcome, for the bikers could not bring themselves to continue fighting. Angels, after all, did not hit one another. Angels were pure and serene and heavenly and holy.

Hopelessly confused, the biker-angels began batting out.

Jax scuttled again, and found himself on the deck of the whaling ship as it lurched ponderously across that turbulent, icy-grey ocean.

At the prow, whaling enthusiasts in their bright-orange waterproofs were taking it in turns to fire the harpoon gun.

The specktioneer was giving each of them instructions on how to aim, how to keep the harpoon gun trained on the target while the ship rose and fell, and how and when to press the trigger. In between shots he would reload the gun with a fresh harpoon.

Again and again, a harpoon sprang from the gun-barrel and blasted into the back of one of the whales with a bloody red impact.

Teeth chattering with the cold, Jax ran through the reverse-incantation, DOVE to ROOK. This time he scarcely made a single mistake with the words. He flipped the bird inside-out, and as the rook reappeared in his hands, he heard the whaling enthusiasts' gleeful cries change to murmurs of consternation and then to yelps of alarm.

The whales that had not yet been harpooned were turning around and heading for the ship. The ones that had been harpooned and were still attached to the ship by cables began swimming, in a group, to starboard.

The unharpooned whales gathered by the ship's port side and began butting it with their massive heads.

With one set of whales pulling it and the other set pushing, slowly the whaling ship began to tip over.

The whaling enthusiasts shrieked and screamed as they slithered down the tilting deck. They clutched desperately at anything they thought they might be able to hold on to, but everything on the deck was slippery-slick with sea-water and their fingers could not get a grip. One after another they slid down, fetching up with a bump against the starboard railing.

The deck continued to tilt at an increasingly steep angle.

Jax, steadying himself against the starboard railing, grinned.

Then the whaling enthusiasts started falling overboard,

plunging into the churning grey waves and surfacing moments later, bobbing up like bright-orange buoys.

As the whales continued to turn the whaling ship over, it began to sink sideways. Jax, no longer able to maintain his balance, decided that now was a sensible time to move on to the next zone. Glote had said that the anti-scuttle virus was good for six presses of the button. That meant Jax would pass through three more zones before he was returned to Realworld.

He and the Swami's rook/dove were causing some wonderful havoc in Davy Jones's Locker. With any luck, Net-users would think twice before visiting here again, and also warn their friends not to.

Next stop – the carnival.

J Edgar Glote was sitting in his solar-powered Volvo, which he had parked at the end of the winding road that led up to the Hamlyn residence. He was admiring the view of Los Angeles and dreaming of the day when he, too, would be able to afford to live in a *really* smart neighbourhood like this one, way above the throng and bustle of the city, in a big house crammed with all sorts of lavish furnishings and luxuries. It wouldn't be long. The Net was well on its way to becoming a viable rival to the Web. It already had the edge on the Web in terms of improved graphics and reduced Websickness, but these were minor advantages. Webware programmers would soon catch up. There was one thing, however, which the Net had and which the Web would never have – Davy Jones's Locker. *That* was the Net's ace-in-the-hole. A place where you could indulge in activities that most people frowned on. A land of do-as-you-please.

Yes, things were looking pretty good for the Net and for J Edgar Glote, especially now that he had the Hamlyn brat in his pocket. Jerry 'Jax' Hamlyn was a useful insurance

policy, in case Larry Hamlyn ever found out what was
going on inside – or, geographically speaking, *below* – the
Net. Were Hamlyn ever to learn about Davy Jones's Locker,
he would probably get all ethical and disapproving and
threaten to pull the financial plug on Mesh Inc. But then
all Glote would have to do was tell him that his own son
had visited Davy Jones's Locker, and he had the subscrip-
tion records to prove it. How would *that* look on the TV
news? *Multimillionaire's Son Bats Into Illegal Zones*. CNN
and Pravda International would have a field day. Hamlyn
would have no choice but to let Davy Jones's Locker
continue as it was.

Yes, no matter which way you looked at it, J Edgar Glote's
future was looking very bright indeed. As bright as the
sunny, cloudless sky that arched over Los Angeles in front
of him.

Glote's musings were interrupted by a voice from the
Volvo's dashboard.

'Edgar,' it said, in soft, seductive, feminine tones with
a Swedish accent. 'I have an incoming emergency
message for you. It's being patched through from your
home.'

'Origin?'

'Davy Jones's Locker. There's been some kind of disturbance in Sectors 11 and 3. Users have been scuttling *en
masse*. Some undetermined factor is causing a software
dysfunction. Oh, apparently it's happening in a third sector
now. Sector 18. The whaling-ship scenario.'

'Can it be contained?' Glote asked, keeping his voice
controlled and even. It was nothing to be worried about, he
told himself. A bug of some sort. Maybe a rogue cyberat
that had snuck across into the Net from the Web.

'It appears to be moving between zones in a pattern that
accords with the path of your anti-scuttle virus.'

'What?' exclaimed Glote. 'Give me the user-designation.'

There was a pause. Then the voice said, 'The user-designation is *Jax*.'

'No!' yelled Glote, pounding the steering wheel with the heel of his hand. 'It can't be!'

'I'm afraid so, Edgar,' said the Volvo's in-car AI personality. 'And please calm down.'

'That ungrateful, little, no-good—!' growled Glote. 'Well, I'll sort him out. Nobody interferes with J Edgar Glote's plans! Nobody!'

'Start!' he instructed, and the ignition system, recognizing his voice, started the engine.

'Apply containment procedures,' he said to the car through clenched teeth.

'Understood.'

Glote executed a U-turn and drove back up the road towards the Hamlyn residence.

On the way, he opened the dashboard glove compartment and reached inside for something he kept concealed behind a false panel.

Something he kept there in case of emergencies.

Jax had no idea how switching the rook back, yet again, to the dove would affect the carnival zone. Nor did he have the chance to find out.

He arrived at the carnival to find, standing in front of him, the barker who had lured him into the shooting gallery yesterday. The barker was flanked by two of the thuggish roustabouts.

Jax fumbled with the rook, and managed to blurt out, 'ROOK, ROCK, RACK—' but got no further than that. The roustabouts lunged at him and grabbed his arms. As they pinned his arms to his sides, the startled rook cawed and flew from his grasp. The barker caught the rook in mid-air, clutched its head in one hand and its body in the other, and, without a moment's hesitation, wrung the bird's neck with a hideous snap-crackle-and-pop of bones. He let the limp, dead rook drop to the ground.

Then he took a step towards Jax and bent down until his Glote-like face was directly in front of Jax's face.

'You ain't going nowhere, kid,' the barker said. 'You're staying right where you are until someone in Realworld reaches you and deals with you there.'

Flygirl detected movement out of the corner of one of her surveillance-camera eyes.

A car was pulling up at the front gates of the house. It came to a halt alongside a small brick pillar that stood beside the driveway, a couple of metres in front of the gates. Set on top of the pillar was a video-entryphone panel, with a bell-button and a number-pad.

The driver's-side window of the car slid down. A hand emerged and punched out a five-digit code on the number-pad. The gates swung inwards and the car drove through.

The house CPU registered the number as the personal access-code belonging to J Edgar Glote.

What was Glote doing there? Flygirl wondered. She continued to observe.

Glote's car travelled up the driveway and stopped outside the front door. Flygirl activated the surveillance camera mounted just above the door's fanlight.

Glote switched off the car's engine. She watched him climb out of the car and ascend the short flight of steps that led up to the front door. He was hiding something inside the flap of his jacket, and looked agitated and furtive.

Flygirl made the camera zoom in on the object Glote was holding inside his jacket. She couldn't quite make out what it was.

With his free hand, Glote tapped his personal access-code into the number-pad set into the door frame.

As the door opened, Glote pulled out what he had been keeping inside his jacket.

It was a revolver.

Flygirl looked on in helpless disbelief as Glote, his face a mask of murderous intent, strode into the house.

CHAPTER ELEVEN

HOUSEKEEPING

Flygirl quickly assessed the situation. Jax was in his Webroom, suited up and totally unaware that Glote was in the building. Her friend was in mortal danger, and it was up to her to save him.

She would have to pull out of the house CPU, and somehow get a message through to the Los Angeles Police Department that a murder was about to be committed. But in the time it took her to bat out, take off her Websuit, get the relevant videophone number from International Directory Enquiries and call the LAPD, it would probably be too late. Jax would already be dead. And that was assuming the LAPD believed her and didn't think she was just some crank-caller playing a practical joke.

No, she would have to stop Glote herself. But how? As long as she was inside the house CPU, she was powerless.

Or was she?

Thinking fast, Flygirl located the burglar alarm in the CPU. The alarm was designed to come on automatically when the house was empty. It was connected to the nearest police precinct station, which was down on Sunset Boulevard, a couple of miles away.

She activated it. A signal sped along the wires to the police station, alerting the police computer to a possible break-in at the Hamlyn residence. Within the house itself, however, no bells rang and no lights flashed. This was so that any burglar who inadvertently tripped the alarm would not know he had done so until the police arrived to catch him red-handed.

Flygirl didn't know how long the police would take to get there. It all depended how close-by the nearest squad car was. According to the CPU, the response time could be as much as five minutes. Too long. Jax would be dead by then.

Via a camera in the hallway ceiling, she watched Glote cock the hammer on his revolver and start tiptoeing stealthily across the floor.

Then she noticed a Dyson-drone in one corner of the hallway. The drone was humming happily along, siphoning up dust through its nozzle-snout.

She recalled Jax telling her once about the day of the Webcrash, when the entire house and all its automated appliances had gone crazy.

And suddenly she had an idea.

Glote was halfway across the hallway when something collided with his left ankle. Hard.

Pain shot up from his tarsal bone. He yelped and hopped up and down on his right leg, massaging the spot where he had been hit.

Looking down, he saw the Dyson-drone bumbling away from him with its nozzle-snout waving in the air like a triumphant elephant's trunk.

'Damn hunk of junk!' he hissed. 'You're not supposed to bump into people. You're supposed to avoid us.'

He put his left foot gingerly back down on the floor and tested the ankle. It worked, but there would probably be a large bruise on it tomorrow morning.

Now to get on with what he had come here to do – sort out the Hamlyn brat.

He had already planned how he was going to get away with murdering the little troublemaker. He was going to shoot him, and then dispose of the revolver where no one could find it. He would smash a window from the outside, so that it would look like somebody had broken into the house. Then he would summon the police and tell them that he had arrived at the house to find poor Jerry Hamlyn already dead. He would feign tearful distress. 'If only,' he would say, 'I had arrived a couple of minutes earlier . . .'

The security system was inactive. There would be no recorded evidence. No one would ever know it was he who had committed the deed.

Glote tightened his grip on the revolver and resumed his stealthy progress across the hallway, heading for the corridor that led to the Webroom.

The Dyson-drone came whirring at him again and struck him, this time on the shin.

'Ouch!' cried Glote. He spun round furiously and aimed a kick at the little robotic domestic appliance. The Dyson-drone darted backwards to avoid his foot.

Another drone came hurtling at Glote from the living-room doorway. It was a sweeper, with a brush attachment on the end of an articulated stalk. It rammed the brush-head into Glote's right buttock.

'Ouch!' cried Glote again. He grabbed for the brush attachment but the sweeper took evasive action and jabbed the brush-head into Glote's other buttock.

'OUCH!' cried Glote yet again.

Suddenly, it seemed as if he was being set upon by every cleaning-drone in the house. They came at him from all directions like a miniature tank battalion converging on a military target. Polishers and dusters and waxers and wipers surrounded and assaulted him with their various cloths, pads, brushes, and spinning scrubbers.

Glote reeled this way and that as the drones subjected him to a succession of blows to the legs and pelvis (none of them could reach any higher than Glote's waist). He lashed out with his feet in retaliation. Some of his kicks connected, sending drones skidding across the floor, but mostly the drones were too quick for him. Glote could scarcely believe what was happening. It was as if the entire house had gone mad!

Finally, he managed to battle his way through the encircling drones and stumble away. Flygirl sent the drones off after him in a pack.

He staggered into the kitchen, and ordered the door to close behind him.

Flygirl made the door refuse to obey, no matter how many times and how insistently Glote gave the *close* command.

The drones piled through the open doorway, brandishing their implements and attachments like an angry mob.

Glote scrambled up onto one of the kitchen counters, wincing at the pain this caused his bruised, battered legs. He levelled his gun at the drones and shouted, 'Back off! Back off or I'll shoot!'

Naturally, the threat did not perturb the drones in the slightest. They clustered at the foot of the counter in a whirring, whining, whirling throng.

Then the kitchen door slid shut.

Glote looked at the door in abject despair. Now he was trapped in a room with dozens of domestic appliances gone berserk. This was a nightmare!

And it wasn't just domestic appliances that had it in for him. Flygirl took command of Jax's PseudoPup, which, until Glote came charging into the kitchen, had been curled up asleep in its basket. The little artificial dog had a remote-control link to the house CPU, so that it could be shut down when the human occupants were out and thus would not drain its batteries needlessly by scampering about when there was no one around to be amused by its antics.

Flygirl had the PseudoPup leap from its basket and bound up onto the counter where Glote had taken refuge. The PseudoPup snarled and bared its teeth at the computer genius. Then it started snapping at Glote's legs with a ferocity that surprised Flygirl. She assumed that, at some point in the past, Glote had done something mean to the PseudoPup, and that as a result, somewhere in its tiny microchip brain the PseudoPup harboured a genuine resentment of Glote. Its programming forbade it to bite anything, but it was offering a very good impersonation of a dog that *could* and *would* bite, given half a chance.

By now Glote was thoroughly rattled. Sweating, eyes bulging, he aimed the revolver wildly around the room, threatening to shoot anything and everything.

Flygirl was glad to see how unnerved Glote had become, but she hadn't yet finished with him. She took control of the thermostat that regulated the ambient temperature in the kitchen and dropped it to well below freezing.

Soon Glote's panting breaths were emerging as chilly clouds. He started shivering. His teeth began to chatter. The sweat on his face turned to a crust of ice. A drip of clear mucus collected at the tip of his nose and froze to an icicle. His spectacles frosted over. Eventually, his fingers became too numb with cold to hold the revolver, and the gun dropped onto the countertop.

With the PseudoPup still yapping and snapping viciously at him and the cleaning-drones still besieging his perch, Glote sank down to the countertop and huddled himself into a shivering ball.

That was how the police found him a few minutes later.

All this time, Jax was still trapped at the carnival, completely oblivious of all that was going on in the house. The roustabouts had a good firm grip on his arms, so there was no way he could scuttle or bat out. The Glote-like barker was pacing to and fro in front of him, muttering vague threats.

'Maybe we could put you on show,' the barker said at one point. '*The Poor Little Rich Kid*. That'd give everyone a good laugh.'

Jax barely paid any attention. He was too busy worrying about what might be going to happen to his body in Realworld. Glote couldn't be planning to kill him, could he? Surely not. But what else could the barker have meant when he had said that someone was on his way in Realworld to deal with him?

A familiar and distinctive voice from behind him interrupted his thoughts.

'I sHalL WArN YoU genTLeMEn OncE, AnD ONCe onLy. STAnd AWaY fRom tHE BoY aND no HaRm WiLl CoME tO YoU.'

Jax turned his head round as far as it would go.

Sure enough, it was the Swami.

The Swami offered Jax a brief but reassuring smile, and then returned his attention to the roustabouts. 'WeLL?' he said.

'And just who in heck are *you*?' demanded the barker. 'You sure as hell don't sound like you come from round these parts.'

'WhERe i cOme fROm, YOu cANnoT poSsIBly IMagIne. ALl YOu NeeD knOW aBouT ME iS thAT i Am a FRieND oF thIS boY.'

'Well, lucky him,' the barker drawled sarcastically. 'Now buzz off back to India or wherever it is you turban-wearing types live. This here's got nothing to do with you. This is between me and the boy.'

The Swami sighed. 'DoN'T sAy i DidN'T WArN yoU.'

He raised his hands and made a series of quick, delicate gestures in the air as though he were manipulating a set of tiny invisible controls. Arcane energy crackled at his fingertips. Then a ball of light manifested around each of his hands.

He aimed a hand at each of the roustabouts and sent the two balls of light whizzing at them.

The startled roustabouts had no time to duck. The balls of light hit them simultaneously, and the result was impressive. The roustabouts shattered into millions of pieces like a pair of fragile china statuettes struck by bowling balls. Their powdered fragments sprayed over the grass in two long dusty streaks.

Jax's arms were free. He had never felt so relieved in all his life.

The barker, staring at the remains of the disintegrated roustabouts, sputtered and stuttered. 'That ain't—! I mean, you can't—! I mean, that just ain't—!'

The Swami walked up to him. 'I KnoW YoU aRE jusT a VIRtuAL ConStruCT,' he said. 'i KNoW You HAvE No ConTroL OVEr whAt yoU DO; YOu sIMpLY oBEy YOuR proGRamMiNg. NonETHeLeSS, WHaT yOU dO Is WIckEd, aND tHat MAkEs yOU WIckEd.'

'No, no, you've – you've got me all wrong,' stammered the barker. 'I'm just a showman. I give folks what they want.'

'iF tHaT Is so,' said the Swami, 'THeN YoU wiLl HAVe nO oBJectIon TO WhAt i AM aBOut to dO.'

So saying, the Swami brushed a hand over the barker's face.

Uttering a horrible groan, the barker fell to his knees. Where the Swami's hand had touched him, a lump like a wart appeared. It swelled rapidly until it was the size of a golf ball. Meanwhile, other similar lumps started sprouting around it.

Soon one half of the barker's face was covered in these tumorous growths, and they were spreading down his neck and beneath his shirt-collar to his chest. One of his eyes was puffed shut, and his Derby hat fell off, dislodged from his head by the lumps that had crept up beneath his hair. His groans were terrible to hear, and for all that he hated the barker, Jax couldn't help but feel a little sorry for him, too.

The barker's groaning attracted a small crowd of curious onlookers. It also drew some of the carnival's permanent residents out from their nearby tents.

Out they came, a bizarre selection of outcasts and medical oddities. Three-ton Tess, the Fattest Lady in the World. Bonzo the Dog-faced Boy. Zit-Man the Living Pustule. The Alligator Girl. And many of the other unfortunates who, for want of a better classification, could be called *freaks*. Out they came to join the crowd of onlookers. And the so-called normal people – many of whom had tailored their avatars to disguise certain minor deformities of their own, such as hair-loss and obesity – parted to give the freaks a space all to themselves. And together, the normal people and the freaks watched the barker's gradual transformation. Watched as his clothing tore at the seams and lumps pushed through. Watched as his hands became lost beneath a profusion of swellings. Watched as his entire body became one distended, warty mass, vaguely shaped like a man.

When it was over, the barker was left crouching on the ground, sobbing.

Then the freaks stepped forwards.

A dwarf took hold of the misshapen knot of flesh and skin that was the barker's right hand. Bonzo the Dog-faced Boy took hold of its counterpart on the other side. Together they helped the barker to his feet.

The other freaks surrounded them, and, with a gentle solemnity, the barker was escorted away.

He was one of them now. A freak himself. And that was how he would remain for as long as Davy Jones's Locker survived.

The crowd of onlookers dispersed and drifted away, having seen all there was to see. Jax and the Swami were left alone.

'YOu hAvE Done weLL,' the Swami told Jax. 'a GREaT disRuPtIon haS BeEn CAuSeD. THe rePuTatIon oF daVY jONes'S LOcKer haS BeEn cAst inTo DOubT. I SUsPecT iT WiLL noT ConTInUE TO surVivE In ITs CUrreNT foRM muCh LOngEr.'

'Yeah, well, you had a lot to do with that,' said Jax. He pointed to the dead rook on the ground. 'And so did *it*,' he added regretfully.

The Swami bent down and picked up the bird. Cradling it in his arms, he stroked its body three times.

The rook stirred, opened an eye, and uttered a weak but encouraging caw.

'iT Will REcOVer,' the Swami said. 'IT MeRElY nEeDEd rEboOtinG.'

'Oh no!' Jax exclaimed abruptly, horrified. He had been so caught up in watching the grisly spectacle of the barker's transformation that, incredibly, he had clean forgotten about the danger he was in, in Realworld. 'I've got to leave here right now,' he said to the Swami.

'oNe moMEnT. I hAVe aN iMpoRTanT mESsaGE i MUst cONveY tO yoU. SOmEthINg iS sHortlY goInG tO hapPeN – aN EvEnt tHAT wILL CHangE yoUr eNtirE plANEt.'

'Please, can it wait?'

'wE ArE reVEaliNg ouR PreSEncE onLy To CHiLdreN. CHiLDReN HaVe MORe fLeXibLe MiNds. THEy aDApt anD ACcEpT moRe ReAdiLy tHan ADUltS.'

'I'm serious. I can't hang around.' Jax's finger was poised over his scuttle button.

'lIsTen To ME!' the Swami insisted. 'PLeasE! WE aRE hEre iN greAT nuMberS, anD soON tHeRe is GoinG To Be a TErRiBlE coNFusIon. SOoN WE arE GOinG tO lEAve thiS plACe anD TAkE FlESh. tHE sHocK wIlL bE LesSEnEd iF somE haVe beEn WarNEd in ADVaNce. UNdERstAnd! I Am NoT HUmaN. i AM noT DIgiTal.'

'I'm really sorry. Thanks for everything.'

'I aM—'

Jax scuttled just as the Swami spoke two more words. The two words were almost drowned out by the sound of the batting-out tone. Almost.

Jax wrenched off his Websuit hood. He was alone in his Webroom. He commanded the door to lock itself and open for no one. He was safe!

He plumped himself down on the padded floor, feeling suddenly exhausted. It had been a close-run thing. If the Swami had gone on talking much longer—

A frown crossed Jax's face. The Swami's final two words. What *were* they? What had he been saying?

There was a loud pounding on the Webroom door.

Glote! thought Jax.

He scrambled to his feet and retreated swiftly to the corner of the room furthest away from the door.

The pounding went on.

Then a voice said, 'Jerry? Jerry, are you in there? Are you all right?'

It was his father.

'Yeah, Dad,' said Jax, his voice cracking with relief. 'Yeah. I'm fine.'

'Oh, thank God. Jerry, the police are here with me. We have Glote. They've taken him into custody and he's said he's willing to confess everything. Something kind of peculiar happened to him. The house— I don't know, as far as I can tell, the house *attacked* him. He's completely freaked out by it. I think he might even have gone a little insane. Jerry, can you hear me in there?'

'Yeah, Dad, I can hear you. Will you hold on a moment? I've just got to catch the fade on something.'

'All right. I'll be right here.'

The Swami's final two words . . .

Jax racked his brain. He had heard them, and he knew in the back of his mind that they were highly significant. He *had* to remember what they were.

At last they popped into his head.

And then he had to sit down on the floor again because the implication of those two small words made him dizzy and light-headed.

It couldn't be right. He must have misheard.

But the two words made sense of everything the Swami had said before. They made sense, too, of what Flygirl had observed about the Swami software – the algorithms all back-to-front, the code not being in binary.

Jax shook his head, and smiled, and then began to laugh.

It was crazy, but it could only be true.

The two words were: *aN aLieN*.

The Swami was from outer space. And he wasn't here alone.

CHAPTER TWELVE

GONE FISHING

Three days later, Flygirl was in the BiblioTech, completing her research into utopias (because she never liked to leave a job unfinished), when President Samuel Jackson appeared beside her again and politely begged a moment of her time.

Flygirl looked up from the book she was reading – *News From Nowhere* by William Morris – and sighed testily.

'It'll wait,' she said. 'Whatever it is, it'll wait.'

The President was taken aback. 'I appreciate you're busy,' he said, 'but this is kind of a special occasion.'

'So *you* say,' replied Flygirl, and she hunched over her book again, putting her elbows on the lectern and her face in her fists – the posture of someone very much determined not to be disturbed.

'Well, I guess I *could* come back at a more convenient time, Miss N'Douba,' said the President.

'You do that,' said Flygirl. Then her head snapped round. 'Wait a second. What did you just call me?'

'You *are* Anita N'Douba, right?' said the President. 'Or have I got the wrong person? I gotta admit, this technology stuff gets me pretty confused sometimes.'

Flygirl's jaw dropped. Her mouth gaped. This was one of those rare occasions in her life when she was lost for words.

'You didn't think it was me, did you?' said the avatar of

the President of the United States. 'I get that a lot. Seems some folk've been taking my likeness in vain.'

'But— But—'

The president smiled. 'I heard 'bout what you did the other day, Anita. You and your pal Jerry, Larry Hamlyn's kid. You busted that whole Davy Jones's Locker thing wide open. Quite a feat.'

'But—'

'Saved your friend's life as well. Kept cool as ice in a tricky situation. Came up with a plan. You're a smart kid. I could use someone like you on my staff.'

'But—'

'In an advisory capacity,' the President went on. 'As a kinda Web liaison officer. I'm an old guy, after all, an' frankly I find mosta this Web stuff just a little bit baffling. Your job would be to keep me in touch with what's going on in here. You'd report, once a month, directly to me. Keep me up with the latest developments, the latest innovations. How's that sound?'

'But—'

'One thing, though,' said the President. 'You want the job, Anita, you're going to have to learn to say something else other than "But—"'

Flygirl closed her mouth, breathed in deep through her nose, composed herself, and said, 'I'm your Flygirl, Mr President.'

President Jackson grinned hugely. '*Flygirl*? That's your alias, right? Damn, that's funky! Y'know, I think you an' me, Flygirl, we're gonna make a great team.'

After the president had left, Flygirl was unable to concentrate on her reading any more. She was far too excited. In fact, she kept giggling to herself so much that eventually one of the librarians asked her to leave.

Web Liaison Officer to President Jackson! She couldn't wait to tell Jax about it. He'd burst with envy!

Then she remembered that Jax was incommunicado for the next few days. He was away in the mountains of Oregon . . .

Fishing.

The lake was placid and crystal-clear. Barely a breath of wind disturbed its surface. There were mountain ridges and pine forests all around. The great hiss of Nature's emptiness was all that could be heard.

The small fibreglass rowing-boat floated in the middle of the lake. Jax and his father sat aboard it, side by side. Each had a fishing rod in his hands, and each was gazing contentedly at the spot where his line entered the water, marked by a small, bobbing orange float, the bull's-eye at the centre of a set of concentric ripples. The silence between Jax and his father was companionable. It didn't matter that neither of them had had so much as a nibble on his line all morning. Being there, and the anticipation of a catch, were enough to keep them both happy.

Finally, Jax broke the silence. 'Dad,' he said, 'how long did you know about Davy Jones's Locker?'

'I thought we agreed when we set out on this trip that we weren't going to talk about any of that until we got back home,' said Hamlyn.

'I know, but it's been bugging me.'

'OK,' said Hamlyn, playing out a bit more line into the water. 'A couple of months ago the Webcops contacted me, saying they'd heard unconfirmed rumours of improper activities in the Net. They had a pretty good idea who was responsible, and so did I. Glote. Unfortunately, they couldn't prove anything at the time, so we decided to play a waiting game. We figured that Glote, left to his own devices, would eventually get over-ambitious. That's the kind of guy he is. Then he'd make a mistake, and we would ensnare him. So I kept stringing Glote along, pretending I knew nothing about Davy Jones's Locker so that his suspicions wouldn't be aroused. We needed absolutely watertight evidence if we were going to bring him down, and if he had gotten wind of what we were up to, he'd have shut Davy Jones's Locker down immediately and there'd be nothing to prove it had ever existed.'

'But weren't you worried what people would think? After all, this was going on inside a company *you* owned.'

'The Webcops made it clear that, as far as they were concerned, I was innocent of all involvement in Davy Jones's Locker, and that, if necessary, they would go on record, publicly exonerating me of all blame. And I believe people would think far worse of me if it turned out that I'd known about Davy Jones's Locker and *not* done anything about it.'

This had proved to be true. On the evening after his second bat into Davy Jones's Locker, Jax had watched his father on the TV news giving a statement to reporters, saying that he deplored everything that had gone on in Davy Jones's Locker and that, despite the financial loss he was going to incur, he was decommissioning the Net with immediate effect. From the presenter's comments afterwards, it was clear that opinion of Larry Hamlyn was entirely favourable. He had done the right thing, the decent thing.

Opinion of J Edgar Glote could not have been more different. Flygirl had used the surveillance cameras to record him going through the house with his revolver and being attacked by the cleaning-drones, and cornered in the kitchen. The footage was being shown repeatedly on TV. No one, it seemed, got tired of watching it, and late-night chatshow hosts couldn't stop making jokes about it and about Glote. Being attacked by a house was a fair and just retribution on the man who had attempted to kill Larry Hamlyn's son.

'And, of course,' said Jax, 'you didn't want me batting into the Net because—'

'Because I couldn't risk you winding up in Davy Jones's Locker.' Hamlyn rolled his eyes. 'I should have known that would be the *first* place you went.'

'Why didn't you say anything at the time, though?'

'I couldn't. To keep Glote completely in the dark, I had to pretend to everyone – you included – that I had no idea what was really going on.'

'Well, I wish you *had* told me.'

'Yes, and I wish I'd listened to you when you tried to tell me that you'd been to Davy Jones's Locker. But I was too preoccupied. Things had reached a crucial stage. Remember when I was supposed to be attending a charity fund-raiser? Actually I was in a meeting with the Web-cops. I told them I couldn't hold out much longer. I couldn't keep lying to you, particularly since you'd gotten hold of that junction-box. I told them we had to spring the trap on Glote now, and we were trying to figure out how to do that when the call came through from the LAPD that there'd been a break-in at the house. And not long after that, word came that Glote had been caught on the premises with a gun—' Hamlyn's voice trailed off. The thought of how close Glote had come to killing his son, his only remaining family, was almost too much to bear. 'Well, hey, he's not our problem any more, is he?'

Jax nodded. 'I guess he was right about one thing, though. He said you and I haven't been communicating properly.'

'Maybe so. But I get the feeling that's going to change from now on. Don't you?'

Jax couldn't help but think then of the Swami. If what the Swami had said was true, then a lot more than a father/son relationship was about to change. The entire planet was in for a major shake-up. Mankind was about to have its first encounter with an extraterrestrial race!

Jax wanted to tell everyone, warn everyone what was about to happen, but he knew no one would believe him. It would have to remain his secret. For now.

Hamlyn inhaled a lungful of fresh mountain air and let it slowly out as a sigh.

'It doesn't get much better than this, does it?' he said, gazing around at the spectacular scenery. 'In fact, you and me in this boat, miles from anywhere, in the midst of all this beauty and tranquillity – I'd say this was pretty much perfection. Wouldn't you, Jerry?'

Jax sniffed the air. Suddenly, impossibly, inexplicably, he could smell roses.

'Yeah,' he said. 'Yeah, Dad, I'd say this was utopia.'

WEBSPEAK – A GLOSSARY

AI   Artificial intelligence. Computer programs that appear to show intelligent behaviour when you interact with them.

avatar or realoe   Personas in the Web that are the representations of real people.

basement-level   Of the lowest level possible. Often used as an insult, as in 'You've got a basement-level grasp of the situation.'

bat   The moment of transition into the Web or between sites. You can 'do a bat' or 'go bat'. Its slang use has extended to the everyday world. 'bat' is used instead of 'come in', 'take a bat' is a dismissal. (From *Blue And Tone*.)

bite   To play a trick, or to get something over on someone.

bootstrap   Verb, to improve your situation by your own efforts.

bot   Programs with AI.

chasing the fade   Analysing what has happened in the Web after you have left it.

cocoon   A secret refuge. Also your bed or own room.

cog	Incredibly boring or dull. Initially specific to the UK and America this slang is now in use worldwide. (From *Common Or Garden* spider.)
curl up	'Go away, I don't like you!' (From *curl up and die*.)
cyberat	A Web construct, a descendent of computer viruses, that infests the Web programs.
cybercafe	A place where you can get drinks and snacks as well as renting time in the Web.
cyberspace	The visual representation of the communication system which links computers.
d-box	A data-box; an area of information which appears when people are in Virtual Reality (VR).
download	To enter the Web without leaving a Realworld copy.
down the plug	A disaster, as in 'We were down the plug'.
egg	A younger sibling or annoying hanger-on. Even in the first sense this is always meant nastily.
eight	Good (a spider has eight legs).
flame	An insult or nasty remark.
fly	A choice morsel of information, a clue, a hint.
funnel	An unexpected problem or obstacle.
gag	Someone, or something, you don't like very much, who you consider to be stupid. (From *Glove And Glasses*.)
glove and glasses	Cheap but outdated system for experiencing Virtual Reality. The glasses al-

	low you to see VR, the gloves allow you to pick things up.
Id	Interactive display nodule.
mage	A magician.
mip	Measure of computer power.
nick or alias	A nickname. For example, 'Flygirl' is the nickname of Anita.
one-mip	Of limited worth or intelligence, as in 'a one-mip mind'.
phace	A person you meet in the Web who is not real; someone created by the software of a particular site or game.
phreak	Someone who is fanatical about virtual reality experiences in the Web.
protocol	The language one computer uses to talk to another.
raid	Any unscheduled intrusion into the Web; anything that forces someone to leave; a program crash.
realoe	See *avatar*
Realworld	What it says; the world outside the Web. Sometimes used in a derogatory way.
scuttle	Leave the Web and return to the Realworld.
SETI	Search for Extra-terrestrial Intelligence.
SFX	Special effects.
silky	Swarmy, over enthusiastic, untrustworthy.
six	Bad (an insect has six legs).
slows, the	The feeling that time has slowed down after experiencing the faster time of the Web.
spider	A web construct. Appearing in varying sizes and guises, these are used to pass on warnings or information in the

	Web. The word is also commonly applied to teachers or parents.
spidered-off	Warned away by a spider.
spin in	To enter the Web or a Website.
spin out	To leave the Web or a Website.
strand	A gap between rows of site skyscrapers in Webtown. Used to describe any street or road or journey.
suck	To eat or drink.
supertime	Parts of the Web that run even faster than normal.
TFO	Tennessee Fried Ostrich.
venomous	Adjective; excellent; could be used in reference to piece of equipment (usually a Websuit) or piece of programming.
vets	Veterans of any game or site. Ultra-vets are the *crème de la crème* of these.
VR	Virtual Reality. The illusion of a three dimensional reality created by computer software.
warlock	A sorcerer; magician.
Web	The worldwide network of communication links, entertainment, educational and administrative sites that exists in cyberspace and is represented in Virtual Reality.
Web heads	People who are fanatical about surfing the Web. (See also phreaks.)
Web round	Verb; to contact other Web users via the Web.
Websuit	The all over body suit lined with receptors which when worn by Web users allows them to experience the full physical illusion of virtual reality.

Webware   Computer software used to create and/
                   or maintain the Web.

widow   Adjective; excellent; the term comes
                   from the Black Widow, a particularly
                   poisonous spider.

wipeout   To be comprehensively beaten in a
                   Web game or to come out worse in
                   any Web situation.

OTHER TITLES IN
THE WEB SERIES

GULLIVERZONE by Steve Baxter

February 7, 2027, World Peace Day. It's a day of celebration everywhere. Even access to the Web is free today. It's the chance Sarah's been waiting for, a chance to sample the most wicked sites, to visit mind-blowing virtual worlds. She chooses GulliverZone and the chance to be a giant amongst the tiny people of Lilliput.

But the peace that is being celebrated in the real world does not extend into cyberspace. There is a battle for survival being fought in Lilliput and what Sarah discovers there in one day will be enough to change her life forever – providing she can get out to live it . . .

GULLIVERZONE, the fear is anything but virtual.

GULLIVERZONE ready for access.

FEEL UP TO ANOTHER?
DREAMCASTLE by Stephen Bowkett

Dreamcastle is the premier fantasy role-playing site on the Web, and Surfer is one of the premier players. He's one of the few to fight his way past the 500th level, one of the few to take on the Stormdragon and win. But it isn't enough, Surfer has his eyes on the ultimate prize. He wants to be the best, to discover the dark secret at the core of Dreamcastle.

And he's found the girl to take him there. She's called Xenia and she's special, frighteningly special.

He's so obsessed that he's blind to Rom's advice, to Kilroy's friendship and to the real danger that lies at the core of the Dreamcastle. A danger that could swallow him whole . . . for real.

DREAMCASTLE, it's no fantasy.

DREAMCASTLE ready for access.

THINK YOU'RE UP TO IT?
UNTOUCHABLE by Eric Brown

Life might be easier for most people in 2027 but for Ana Devi, whose only home is the streets of New Delhi, it's a battle for survival. She's certainly never dreamed of visiting the bright virtual worlds of the Web. And when her brother is kidnapped the Web is certainly the last thing she is thinking about. But the Web holds the secret to what has happened to her brother and to dozens of other New Delhi street children.

How can Ana possibly find enough money to access the Web when she can barely beg enough to eat each day? Who will help her when her caste means that no one will even touch her? Somehow she must find a way or she will never see her brother again.

Dare you touch the truth of UNTOUCHABLE?

UNTOUCHABLE ready for access.

TAKE ANOTHER WALK ON THE WILD SIDE
SPIDERBITE by Graham Joyce

In 2027 a lot of schooltime is Webtime. Imagine entering Virtual Reality and creeping through the Labyrinth with the roars of the Minotaur echoing in your ears? Nowhere near as dull as the classroom. The sites are open to all, nothing is out of bounds. So why has Conrad been warned off the Labyrinth site? There shouldn't be any secrets in Edutainment.

Who is behind the savage spiders that swarm around Conrad whenever he tries to enter the site? And why do none of his friends see them? There is a dark lesson being taught at the centre of the Labyrinth . . .

SPIDERBITE, school was never meant to be this scary . . .

SPIDERBITE ready for access.

ARE YOU READY TO GO AGAIN?
LIGHTSTORM by Peter F. Hamilton

Ghostly lights out on the marsh have been the subject of tales and rumours for as long as anyone can remember but the reality is far more frightening than any ghost story. Something is going wrong at the nearby energy company and they are trying to keep it a secret. Somebody needs to be told. But Aynsley needs to do it. The Web keeps him in touch with a network of friends across the world and it might just offer him a way in past the company security to find out exactly what's going on.

But the Web works both ways. If Aynsley can get to the company then the company can get to him. And the company has a way of dealing with intruders.

LIGHTSTORM, sometimes it's best to be in the dark.

LIGHTSTORM ready for access.

IS THIS THE END?
SORCERESS by Maggie Furey

A fierce and menacing intelligence is corrupting the very heart of the Web. Vital research data is being stolen. Someone or something is taking control of a spectacular new gamezone. The Web is no longer safe. The Sorceress continues to outwit all who attempt to destroy her, but her time is running out and she will stop at nothing to get what she wants. Someone must stop her.

Only one person has the power to overcome the awesome creator of the Web.

But who could survive a battle with the Sorceress?

SORCERESS ready for access.

BRACE YOURSELF!
WEBCRASH by Steve Baxter

When the world's computers are overwhelmed by a sudden flood of energy from outer space the Web is hit hard. This is WEBCRASH and unfortunately for Metaphor she's caught in the middle when the barriers between two virtual worlds collapse and the vikings from one are thrown into conflict with a high-tech future criminal from the other.

Trapped in the Web, running out of time, Metaphor has to help the vikings and close the gap between two worlds that were never meant to mix.

WEBCRASH, a collision course with disaster.

WEBCRASH ready for access.

JUST WHEN YOU THOUGHT IT WAS SAFE . . .
CYDONIA by Ken Macleod

Who can you trust in a world full of conspiracy? Links and Weaver used to be bitter game zone rivals in the Web but they are forced to rely on each other when the lies and deceit surrounding the Cydonia conspiracy site begin to spread into the outside world. If you believed everything you'd end up trusting no-one. Caught up in their own tangled web no-one is looking to where the real story is; the stars.

CYDONIA, the truth is nowhere.

CYDONIA ready for access.

A WHITE KNUCKLE RIDE
SPINDRIFT by Maggie Furey

Why has an old enemy come back to haunt Cat and Eleni?
And should they trust a warning from someone that evil?
Soon they have no choice as the threat that has haunted
their dreams spills over into the Web. Is Realworld next? Bit
by bit the story falls into place and the girls find out that
their world doesn't just belong to them. And when that
happens there really is no place to hide.

SPINDRIFT nowhere to run to.

SPINDRIFT ready for access December 1998.